But the light-flirtation idea didn't seem so good as they headed back to the house.

Walking beside him, aware of him in every cell of her body, was torture and Jo felt her tension building and building as they approached the tree where Charles had kissed her.

"I think perhaps we should kiss again, don't you?" he asked as they grew inevitably closer. "Establish a little custom that is just for us?"

And although her nerves were screaming with frustration, her body demanding at least a kiss, she hesitated, suddenly aware that no flirtation with this man would ever be light.

But before she could process this, his hand slid around her waist and he drew her into the deep, hidden shadow beneath the tree, and, unable to resist, she let him. She let him turn her toward him, press her body against his and claim her lips with a kiss that burned through any doubts, and melted her bones so she slumped against him, replete for the moment, although she knew she'd want more.

Need more…

Dear Reader,

It's been a long time since I wrote a prince book, and even then it was a novella for a collection, so it hardly counts. But when I began to think of this story, during torrential rain that seemed to be going on forever, the idea of my characters meeting at such a time—especially when a bucket of water was involved—took root in my head and wouldn't go away. The only thing to do was to try to work out the rest of the story. Knowing a number of adopted children—my sister and her husband adopted five mixed-race babies—and aware of the ambivalence many of them feel toward their birth parents, I realized it could be another thread in the story. The next thing to do was to meet the characters and get to know them, and who better than a charming prince and a hardworking small-town doctor?

I really enjoyed the journey of these characters and hope you will, too.

With best wishes,

Meredith

NEW YEAR WEDDING FOR THE CROWN PRINCE

———

MEREDITH WEBBER

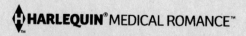

Recycling programs
for this product may
not exist in your area.

ISBN-13: 978-1-335-66384-9

New Year Wedding for the Crown Prince

First North American Publication 2018

Copyright © 2018 by Meredith Webber

Printed in U.S.A.

CHAPTER ONE

CHARLES EDOUARD ALBERT CINZETTI, Crown Prince of Livaroche, gripped the armrest of his seat as the small plane in which he was travelling—foolishly, he now conceded—was tossed around in gale-force winds and lashing rain.

The journey had been interminable: long hours in the air, lengthy delays at foreign airports and now this. The pilot's laconic apology for the rough flight—'Sorry about the bumps, folks, bit of a low off the coast'—had hardly been reassuring, although Charles began to see lights through the rain, growing steadily brighter, and then they were down, with every passenger on board heaving a huge sigh of relief.

Not that Charles's journey had ended. He had to find his way to the seaside town of Port Anooka, another thirty miles from the airport.

'Just down the road,' the travel agent had told him. 'You could hire a car.'

Which had been a good idea back in Sydney,

where the weather was clear and bright, but in this deluge?

No way!

'Just a bit of a low off the coast,' the cab driver told him, as he steered his vehicle through practically horizontal rain. 'Port'll be cut off, and that place you want, the old lady's house on the bluff—well, you won't even be able to get back to the village once the tide comes in and the road floods.'

Charles wondered if it was jet lag that made the conversation—carried out in clear, everyday English words—unintelligible.

A village that was cut off and flooded at high tide?

Coming from a tiny, landlocked principality, he knew little of tides but surely villages were built above high-tide marks?

And what was this low everyone was talking about?

He gathered it was a meteorological depression but he didn't know much about them either. At home, it might mean rain, or in winter snow, but obviously here it brought a deluge and wild wind.

'The old lady's barmy, ya know,' the driver continued, breaking into Charles's consideration of the limits of his very expensive education. 'Livin' out there on her own, the place fallin' to bits around her.'

Place falling to bits? Charles thought. He thought of the comfortable apartment he'd left behind at the palace. Of the snow, already deep on the mountain slopes, and Christmas lights slung along the streets; rugged-up carollers knocking on doors, and the city's Christmas tree ready to be raised into pride of place in the city square.

Had he made a mistake, coming here?

But how else could he get to know at least something of the mother who'd died giving birth to him—the woman his father had loved, married and buried, all within eighteen months of meeting her?

His father would talk of how she had made him laugh, how kind she had been to everyone she'd met, and how they'd fallen in love at first sight.

Not much help in putting together a picture of the whole woman, but Charles did know they'd met at Christmas, which was why he'd chosen to come now to see what she'd seen, do what she'd done, and hopefully get to know his grandmother—and to learn why she'd never contacted them. Something his father had never been able to explain—or perhaps had not wanted to explain.

As far as Charles was concerned, someone as loving and giving as his mother—gleaned from his father's description of her—must have grown up in a warm, loving family. He wasn't personally familiar with normal families, but anyone who'd worked in children's wards in a hospital had seen loving families up close, and knew they existed. Not in every case, of course, but in enough to have learnt how strong the bonds of family love could be.

His father had encouraged him to come, perhaps hoping once his son had it out of his system, he'd settle down, marry and have the children so important to the continuation of the royal line.

Charles sighed.

It wasn't that he didn't want to marry, but no woman he had ever met had made him feel the way his parents must have felt when they'd run away together.

'Port Anooka!' the driver announced, breaking into his thoughts as they entered another lit-up area. 'Not that there's much of it these days, and you're still ten minutes from the house.'

He half turned.

'Sure you want to go out there? Look how high the tide is already. You won't get back in an hour.'

Charles peered through the streaming windshield and was startled to see huge waves crashing onto the promenade along the foreshore, not a hundred yards from the cab.

Was he sure?

Shouldn't he book into a hotel, and perhaps go out tomorrow?

But the journey had already been too long.

'Of course,' he said, hoping the words sounded more positive than he felt. He'd come all this way, so there was no turning back.

Not now he was so close…

Besides, there, ahead of him, was the house, rising up two stories, high on a bluff above the ocean, looking for all the world like something out of a horror film, wreaths of sea mist wisping around it in a temporary lull in the rain.

He paid the driver, thanked him for his further warning of being stuck out here on the bluff, grabbed his hold-all, and headed for the two low steps leading up to the front door.

He'd barely raised his hand to knock when the door flew open and a bucket of water was tossed onto him.

Barmy old lady?

He knew that in England barmy meant a bit mad.

But was she really mad, and this her way of repelling intruders?

Perhaps not as good as the boiling oil of olden days, but still reasonably effective as it had sent him tripping backwards into a large puddle at the bottom of the steps.

He struggled to his feet, still clutching his bag, and faced his opponent.

But the thrower wasn't an old lady. She was a heavily pregnant woman, surely close to giving birth, who was turning away from him, shouting up the stairs to some unseen inhabitant.

'Of course you knew the roof was leaking, Dottie. Why else would you own twelve buckets?'

She was swinging the door shut when she must have caught a glimpse of him, hesitantly approaching the bottom step, drenched in spite of the umbrella he still held with difficulty above his head.

'Who are you? Where did you come from? What are you doing here?' A slight pause in the questions, then, 'You're wet!'

He watched realisation dawn on her face and saw her try to hide a smile as she said, 'Oh, no, did I throw the water over you? You'd better come in.'

'What is it? Who's there?'

The querulous questions came from above— nothing wrong with the barmy old lady's hearing apparently.

'It's just some fellow I threw water at,' the woman yelled back, not bothering to hide her smile now.

She was gorgeous, Charles realised. Tall, statuesque, carrying her pregnancy with pride. And the condition suited her, for her auburn hair shone and her skin was a clear, creamy white tinged with the slightest pink of embarrassment across high cheekbones.

'Don't let him in,' came the instruction from on high, but it was too late. He was already standing, dripping, in the black and white tiled entry, watching the woman disappear into the darkness beyond.

She returned with a large towel, but as she handed it to him she laughed and shook her head.

'That won't do, will it? You're drenched. Come through, there's a bathroom off the kitchen—a little apartment from the days when the house had servants. Mind the bucket! Have you dry clothes in your bag or shall I find something for you?'

Of course he'd have dry clothes in his bag, Jo thought, but she was in such a muddle she barely knew what she was saying. It was shock, that was what it was! Opening the door to find a man standing there—a man at whom she'd just hurled a bucket of water. A man so stunningly attractive even her very pregnant body felt the heat of attraction.

And Dottie was probably right, she shouldn't have let him in. But he'd been drenched, and he didn't *look* like an axe murderer.

In fact, even wet, he was the visual representation of tall, dark and handsome.

Was she out of her mind?

Tall, dark and handsome indeed.

All this was flashing through her head as she

led him through the kitchen to the minuscule bathroom beyond.

'Servants obviously didn't get many luxuries,' she said as she waved him through the door and watched him duck his head to get in.

Which was when she recovered enough common sense to realise she had no idea who the man was!

Or why he was here!

Well, she could hardly ask now, as he'd shut the door between them, and she was *not* going to open it when he was doubtless undressing.

Or think about him undressing…

She didn't do men—not any more, not seriously…

She shook away painful memories of that long-ago time when a man had betrayed her in the worst possible way.

Had being pregnant brought those memories back more often?

Think of this man. The stranger. The here and now.

She'd ask his name later.

The growling noise of the stair lift descending told her Dottie had tired of waiting for an answer and was coming to see what was going on for herself.

Jo hurried back through the kitchen, meeting Dottie in the hall.

'Who is it? What's going on?' the old lady demanded.

'It's a man,' Jo explained. 'He was on the doorstep and I didn't see him as I emptied the bucket. He was soaking wet so I've put him in the downstairs bathroom to dry off.'

'You invited him in?'

Incredulous didn't cut it. The words indicated total disbelief.

'Dottie, he was wet. I'd thrown a bucket of water over him, on top of whatever rain he'd caught getting to the house.'

'He had an umbrella!' Dottie retorted, pointing to where the large black umbrella stood in a pool of water in a corner of the hall.

Jo took a very deep breath and changed the subject.

'I need to check the buckets upstairs,' she said. 'According to the radio reports, the weather is going to get worse.'

Better not to mention that the road to the village was likely to be cut, and the man, whoever he was, might have to stay the night.

Would have to stay the night most probably!

'You can't leave me down here with your stranger,' Dottie told her.

He's hardly *my* stranger, Jo thought, but said, 'Well, come back upstairs with me. I've just emptied the one down here.'

She waved her hand towards the bucket responsible for all the trouble.

Dottie glared at her for a moment, five feet one of determined old lady, then gave a huff and stalked into the living room, which was bucket-free as there were bedrooms or bathrooms above most of the downstairs rooms.

'I won't be long,' Jo promised, taking the stairs two at a time, glad she'd continued her long walks up and down the hills around the village right through the pregnancy.

There were six buckets upstairs and she emptied them all into the bath before replacing them under the leaks. How Dottie slept through the constant drip, drip, drip she didn't know. For herself, too uncomfortable to sleep much anyway, the noise was an almost welcome distraction through the long nights.

She was back downstairs when their visitor returned to the hall.

'I left my wet clothes over the shower, if that's all right,' he said, his beautiful, well-bred, English accent sending shivers down Jo's spine.

'That's fine,' she said, 'although I could put them in a plastic bag for you if you like, because you really should be going. The road to the village will be cut off any minute. The weather bureau's warning that the place will flood at high tide.'

'So everyone keeps telling me,' the stranger said with a smile that made Jo's toes tingle.

But Dottie was made of sterner stuff. Ensconced in her high-backed armchair in the living room, she made her presence known with an abrupt, 'Fiddle-faddle! Stop flirting with the man, Joanna, and bring him in here. If he had any manners he'd have introduced himself before he came through the door.'

Jo shrugged and waved her hand towards the inner door.

'After you,' she said, smiling at the thought of the diminutive Dottie coming up against the stranger.

'Who are you?' Dottie demanded, and Jo watched as the man pulled a chair up close to Dottie and sat down in it, so he was on a level with her, before replying.

'I'm Charles,' he said. 'And I believe I'm your grandson.'

His voice was gentle, so hesitant Jo felt a rush of emotion that brought a wetness to her eyes. Pregnancy sentimentality!

She held her hand to her mouth to stop her gasp escaping, and waited for Dottie to erupt.

She didn't have to wait long.

'Are you just?' Dottie retorted. 'And I'm supposed to believe you, am I? You turn up here with your fancy voice and good shoes and expect what? That I'll leave you my house?'

Trust Dottie to have checked his shoes, Jo thought. Dottie was a firm believer that you could judge a person by his or her shoes...

'No,' Charles was saying politely. 'I wanted to know more about my mother and her family— my family—and you seemed like the best person to tell me.'

'You can't ask her?'

Not a demand this time, but a question asked through quivering lips, as if the answer was already known.

The stranger hesitated, frowning as if trying to make sense of the question, or perhaps trying to frame an answer.

Maybe the latter, for he leant a little closer.

'I'm so very sorry but I thought you'd been told. She died when I was born.'

The words were softly spoken, the stranger bowing his head as he said them, but Jo was more concerned with Dottie, who was as white as the lace collar on her dress.

But even as Jo reached her side, Dottie rallied.

'So, who's your father? No doubt that lying vagabond she ran away with. I suppose you've proof of this!'

If the man was disturbed by having his father labelled this way, he didn't show it.

'My father is Prince Edouard Alesandro Cinzetti. We are from a tiny principality in Europe, a place even many Europeans do not know. It is called—'

'Don't tell me!' Dottie held up her hand. 'I've heard it all before. Some place with liver in the name, or maybe the vagabond's name had liver in it.'

'Liver?' Jo repeated faintly, totally gobsmacked by what was going on before her eyes.

The stranger glanced up and smiled.

'Livaroche,' he said, imbuing the word with all the magic of a fairy-tale.

But Jo's attention was back on Dottie, who seemed to have shrunk back into the chair.

'Go away, I don't want you here,' she said, so feebly that Jo bent to take her arm, feeling for a pulse that fluttered beneath her fingertips.

'Perhaps if you could wait in the kitchen. This has been a shock for Dottie. I'll settle her back in bed and make us all some supper.'

Dottie flung off Jo's hand and glared at the visitor.

'You can't stay here!' she said. 'If you *are* the vagabond's son, next thing I know you'll be making sheep's eyes at my Jo, and whispering sweet nothings to *her*.'

Dark eyes turned towards Jo, his gaze taking

in her bloated figure, and the man had the hide to smile before he answered Dottie.

'Oh, I think someone's already whispered sweet nothings to Jo, don't you?'

The rogue!

But he'd turned her way again, serious now, frowning.

'That's if you are Jo! I'm sorry, we didn't meet—not properly. You know I'm Charles, and you are?'

His aunt? Charles wondered, though why that thought upset him he didn't want to consider.

No, Dottie had said 'my Jo', but it was impossible she could be Dottie's daughter. Dottie must be touching ninety, and if Jo was much over thirty he'd eat his hat.

Maybe a cousin...

But the statuesque beauty was talking.

'I'm Jo Wainwright, local GP in Port Anooka. I took over the practice a couple of years ago, but I have a locum there at present.'

'Then why are you here? Is D— my grandmother ill?'

Somehow saying Dottie seemed far too informal—inappropriate really.

Jo was shaking her head, the red in her hair glinting in the lamplight.

'Dottie is probably the fittest eighty-five-year-old it's ever been my pleasure to meet. She's also the stubbornest—' She broke off to smile at the old woman. 'And she's not entirely steady on her feet, while as for the stair lift—you'd swear she was taking off for Mars, the speed she roars up the stairs on it.'

'Fiddle-faddle!'

Charles ignored the interruption.

'So?'

But again it was Dottie who answered.

'Oh, she thinks I'm not safe to be out here on my own, and she knows darned well I won't move to one of those nasty places where old people rot away and die, so now she spends all her spare time here, eating me out of house and home, and leaving spies here during the week to report back to her.'

As the words were warmed by fondness, and Dottie was clinging to Jo's hand as she spoke, Charles knew it was only bluster, and understood there was a special bond between the pair.

'Dottie's right,' Jo told him. 'I don't like her being out here on her own, but I've grown to love the place almost as much as she does, so staying out here when I can is no hardship.'

She paused, looking a little rueful as she added, 'Mind you, I didn't know about the roof. I keep asking Dottie what needs maintenance and although we've done a bit, there's been a long dry spell so the roof didn't get a mention.'

She had such an animated face the words seemed to come alive as she spoke them, but he could hardly keep staring at her, any more than he could ask her what her husband thought of this arrangement.

So he watched as she spoke quietly to Dottie, helping her to her feet.

'I usually take Dottie her supper in bed. Would you excuse us?'

For the first time, he actually took in the long Chinese robe the older woman was wearing. Had she been settled in bed when he'd arrived and thrown them both into confusion?

'Can I be of assistance?' he offered, and was rewarded with a ferocious scowl from the woman he'd come so far to meet.

'You've caused quite enough drama for one day, thank you very much. You'd best be getting back to the village and we can discuss your visit in the morning.'

'The tide, Dottie,' Jo said gently. 'He won't be able to get back to the village now. He'll have to stay the night.'

'Then put him in the front room,' Dottie said, with such malicious glee Charles knew it was either haunted or, more prosaically, lay beneath the worst of the roof damage.

Left on his own, Charles prowled around the room, aware through all his senses that his mother had once walked here, sat here, maybe helped decorate the ragged imitation tree that stood forlornly in one corner. The need to know more about her had brought him all this way.

He tried to imagine her living in this house, but his thoughts turned to Jo, and it was she he pictured in his mind, maybe on a ladder, laughing as she tried to fix a star to the pathetic tree.

He closed his eyes, replacing Jo's image with one of his mother that he had only formed from pictures, and the stories his father would tell. Would Dottie tell him more stories, the ones he'd come so far to hear? Stories of his mother as a child, her likes and dislikes, anything at all to turn her into a living person instead of a picture by his bed.

It had been close to Christmas back then, too, some annual event having brought his father to the tiny seaside town, and he knew it was a degree of silly sentimentality to have come now, to find out what he could before he married and settled down, taking some of the burden of official duties from his father.

Had his mother prowled the room as he now prowled, arguing with herself—or her parents—about leaving with the lying vagabond?

He knew that had to be his father, because neither of them had ever loved another. And a vagabond he might have been, only even then, Charles was sure, he'd have been called a backpacker. Travel had been something his father had been determined to do, the only time *he'd* ever argued with *his* parents. But although it had disturbed his relationship with them, he'd known he had to see something of the world, to mix with ordinary people, the kind of people he would one day rule.

He himself had done much the same, he realised, when he'd insisted on studying medicine in Edinburgh, with men and women from all layers of society. Eton had been all very well for an education, but he knew how his fellow students had thought and how that layer of society worked. He'd needed to know everyday people.

Even back home for holidays, he'd worked in bars and cafés in the summer, and been a ski instructor in the winter.

But getting back to his father...

A *lying* vagabond?

Jo returned before he had time to consider the word Dottie had used, bringing light into the gloomy room with her smile.

'Been looking for memories of your mother?' she said. 'I've done the same, but sadly never found a thing.'

She paused, then added, 'Though I don't pry to the extent of going through drawers. I wouldn't take advantage of Dottie that way, but I do shake out the books I borrow to read, just in case there's a photo been left to mark a page.'

Charles looked at the wall of books at the back of the room and shook his head. It would take for ever...

'Has she not spoken of her to you?' he asked.

Jo shook her head.

'Not a word, and apparently there's enough solidarity in the village that no one else ever talks about her. I know there has to be a reason because although Dottie's a bit eccentric—well, pretty eccentric—she's not irrational.'

She sighed, shook her head, and bent over to pick up a glass bauble from a box of decorations that stood by the tree, hanging it on a low branch before turning back to Charles.

'Dottie and I usually have grilled cheese on toast for supper, but if you haven't had dinner and would like something more substantial, there are lamb cutlets and plenty of salad things.'

Charles shook his head.

'Grilled cheese on toast sounds fantastic. Takes me back to student days when it was one of the few things I could cook—cheese on toast, beans on toast, eggs on toast!'

That won another smile, which was so open and honest and full of good humour that it caught at something in his chest—just a hitch, nothing more...

You *cannot* be attracted to a very pregnant stranger, he told himself as he followed her to the kitchen, narrowly missing the bucket in the entry.

But the sway of her hips mesmerised him…

It had to be abstinence. How long since he'd been with a woman? The experience of the match his father had promoted, with a young woman who had a very dubious family connection to the old Russian royalty, had been enough to put him off women for life.

Well, for several months at least!

She'd been nice enough, attractive enough, but her conversation began and ended with horses and although he quite liked horses and rode occasionally himself, as a conversational topic, they were way down his list of favourites.

He doubted the woman with the swaying hips would talk horses.

'There's the toaster, and the bread's in the cupboard underneath it. You can do the toast while I grate the cheese. I think it melts better grated. Do you like relish or chutney under the cheese? My dad used to slice up pickles under his.'

Jo only just stopped herself from explaining how her mother had liked Vegemite, and she herself didn't mind the pickles. After all, there was only so much conversational mileage you could get out of grilled cheese on toast. And it had all been a very long time ago.

The memory of that time made her shudder—so much sadness, so much despair and emptiness and loss.

Don't think about it now—concentrate on toast but don't babble on.

She was embarrassed, that was why she'd been talking so much and there were no points for guessing why!

This man's presence—or perhaps her own hyper-awareness of him—was embarrassing her. For some peculiar reason, she'd felt his eyes on her as she'd walked to the kitchen. Not casually on her, but studying her, although that was ridiculous. She'd been imagining things. Why would a man like him be studying a slightly damp, very untidy, very pregnant woman like her?

For a start, being thirty-eight weeks pregnant would announce her as unavailable!

She hauled butter and cheese out of the refrigerator, then milk for Dottie's cocoa, relish in case Charles wanted it, the bottle of pickled gherkins to slice for under *her* cheese, set it all on the scrubbed wooden table in the centre of the big kitchen, then turned to their guest.

He was waggling the handles on the doors of the toaster.

'You realise I'm touching something my mother probably touched. This toaster has to be at least fifty years old.'

Jo grinned at him.

'At least,' she agreed, 'and it doesn't flip open when the toast is done so you have to stand there and watch it and open it before it burns then turn it to do the other side.'

He gave her a 'can you believe it' look and a shake of his head before turning to watch his toast.

Setting the grill in the oven—which was probably older than the toaster—to high, Jo grabbed the grater and a wooden board and began her job.

And if she glanced at their visitor from time to time it was only to see he wasn't burning the toast.

Wasn't it?

He'd found plates and soon delivered a pile of perfectly browned toast to the table.

Toast done, she set him to buttering it—although that meant he was standing close to her, and the discomfort *that* caused had to be because he *was* a stranger...

Surely!

She was slicing gherkins when her belly tightened.

Braxton-Hicks! Her body's practice contractions. She moved a little, knowing that usually stopped them, and kept grating. Charles was now piling grated cheese on the toast he'd buttered.

'I've done two slices each, will that be enough?' he said.

Jo turned to face him, saw a smile lurking in his dark-enough-to-drown-in eyes, and hesitated, her mouth suddenly so dry she couldn't speak.

She had to be imagining whatever it was that was zapping between them.

Had to be!

'You might want more than two slices,' she finally managed, 'and I have sliced pickles under my cheese.'

'Like father, like daughter,' he teased, and she blessed the distraction of another twinge in her belly.

She would hate to think she was *anything* like her father...

Although maybe that was unfair. He'd been a good and loving father up until her mother had died and it probably hadn't been his fault he'd gone to pieces then...

Charles had turned away to put more bread in the toaster, apparently deciding he might need more than two slices, and Jo used the respite from his presence to slide the cheese-laden slices under the grill.

The extra hormones that pregnancy had sent spinning through her body—they must surely be the cause of her...

Her what?

Distraction, she decided, and said it firmly enough in her head to pretend she meant it.

Well, it could hardly be anything more than that, now, could it? She'd seen tall, dark and handsome men before and had never felt the slightest attraction, and so what if his broad shoulders curved in to a neat waist, and his jeans clung to neat buttocks?

She heated milk on the stove for Dottie's cocoa, vowing for the fiftieth time she'd buy a microwave for the house next time she was in town. She put on the kettle for tea and turned to Charles.

'Would you like tea or coffee?'

He smiled—she wished he wouldn't—and said, 'Could I please have cocoa? This has taken me back to student days and it seems right I should be drinking cocoa.'

Jo tore her eyes away from his face. What had she been waiting for, another smile? She poured more milk into the pot on the stove, told the visitor to watch the toast under the grill while she found mugs for the three of them. Even Dottie, to whom tea must be served in fine china cups, drank her cocoa from a mug, and a mug of tea was far more satisfying as far as Jo was concerned.

Charles, who was proving quite proficient in the kitchen, had found more plates and was cutting a couple of bubbling, lightly browned cheese toasts into fingers.

'Two for Dottie, two with pickles for the pregnant lady, and I'll look like a pig eating four, but it seems a very long time since breakfast.'

'You haven't eaten since breakfast?' Jo said in disbelief, but the milk was close to boiling, and she had cocoa to make, so she could hardly pursue the conversation.

Not that Charles—the name was coming more easily into her head—had replied. Instead, he was moving around the kitchen, poking into nooks and crannies, finally finding the trays, hiding in the space beside the ancient refrigerator.

'I'm assuming Dottie has the silver one,' he said, smiling so broadly Jo had to smile back.

'Yes, and slightly better china than you've found there.'

She opened a high kitchen cupboard and produced a fine china plate, bedecked with flowers and edged with gold.

'Just because she's old, she says, she doesn't have to lower her standards,' Jo quoted in explanation.

'Bless her heart!' Charles said, and the phrase must have startled him for he added, very quickly, 'As my nanny would have said.'

Bless her heart indeed!

And a nanny?

No wonder he spoke like an English toff.

Only it wasn't really like that—just beautifully pronounced words that seemed to fill the air with music.

What would it have been like to have been raised like that?

Or even in a normal household.

Another twinge reminded Jo she shouldn't be thinking about the past and definitely not about a man she'd barely met, no matter how pleasant his voice might be.

And weren't Braxton-Hicks contractions supposed to be irregular?

Still, she couldn't think about that now. She'd get the tray up to Dottie, and then…

She didn't know what.

She usually took her tray up and ate in Dottie's bedroom, but would Dottie want the stranger in her bedroom, related though he might be?

And could she, Jo, leave him alone in the kitchen no matter how inhospitable that would seem?

She'd take Dottie's tray up and see what transpired.

Dottie was sitting, propped up on pillows, in the middle of the big bed, the ornately carved bedhead a spectacular backdrop to the minute occupant. Resplendent in her colourful Chinese robe, she was every inch an empress, ready to receive her subjects.

As Jo settled the tray on the small table over Dottie's legs, she said, 'You can bring that man up here to eat his supper. You'll come, of course, so he might as well. We'll grill him, find out what he's up to!'

The last sentence would have startled Jo if she hadn't known Dottie's passion for mystery and detective fiction. Perhaps she'd always nurtured a secret desire to grill someone.

Possibly literally!

'We've been summoned,' she told Charles when she returned to the kitchen, where she found him cutting his extra toast into fingers. He'd also made a pot of tea, though where he'd found the pot she didn't know. 'Do you want sugar in your cocoa?'

'I've already helped myself, but left it to you to pour your own tea how you like it.'

Jo did just that, then lifted her tray and led the way upstairs.

CHAPTER TWO

CHARLES LOOKED AROUND the room, realising that when rain wasn't lashing the windows, Dottie would have an expansive view of the sea from her bed. Here, too, there were the early signs of Christmas decorations—a small, stained-glass decal on one window, a box of tinsel in a corner. Had someone—Jo?—started on the task before the weather turned?

But what really interested him in the room was a chest of drawers to one side of the bed, and the ranks of framed photos taking pride of place across the top of it.

Was there one of his mother?

He could hardly walk over and have a look.

Jo had pulled two chairs closer to the bed from what would be a sitting alcove by the window, and put small side tables beside each of them.

She waved him to one of them, but as she bent to set down her tray, he thought he saw her wince.

Strangers don't ask questions, he told himself, but the doctor in him had to say, 'Are you okay?'

'Practice twinges, that's all,' she said, but the pink had gone from her cheeks and she looked a little drawn.

'I'm also a doctor,' he said to her quietly, 'so if your baby decides to come early, and you can't get into the village, I *have* delivered them before.'

'This baby is *not* coming early,' was the reply, no less forceful for being whispered. 'This is to be a Christmas baby, timed to the minute!'

He considered that a bit ambitious. Would she consider having it induced on Christmas morning if it wasn't showing signs of arrival?

'What are you two whispering about?' Dottie demanded to know.

Charles smiled at her.

'I was just saying it's a coincidence, Jo being a doctor, because that's my profession.'

'Ha!' said Dottie with malicious glee. 'I knew that vagabond was lying!'

Charles shook his head—unable to make any connection.

Jo must have been equally confused, for it was she who asked the question.

'And just why, Dottie, does Charles being a doctor make his father a liar?'

'Because his father always said he was a prince, and if that was true then his son would be a princeling, or whatever a prince's sons are called, and this fellow says he's a doctor.'

She paused, smiling in malicious glee, then went on, 'Although he could be a liar, too, and the doctor thing just humbug!'

'Oh, Dottie,' Jo said, barely able to speak for laughter, 'you do come up with the most startling logic. If his dad's a prince then he's probably one, too, but he could hardly hang around waiting for his father to die so he can have a job. If the liver place is as small as he says it is, there probably aren't enough duties to keep his father busy, let alone Charles as well. He would have needed a job.'

Charles had watched Dottie while Jo was speaking—better by far than watching Jo with the laughter lingering in her eyes. The old lady didn't seem at all perturbed, eating her way through her plate of cheese toast and sipping at her cocoa.

But her eyes were on him the whole time.

Trying to make out if he was the imposter she thought him?

Or trying to see some resemblance to his mother? A family likeness of some kind...

He hoped it was the latter, but after thirty-six years would she be able to tell?

The photos up here would definitely be off limits unless Dottie agreed he could look at them.

There'd been no obvious photos of his mother in the parts of the house he'd seen so far. And, like Jo, he didn't want to pry into drawers.

But he had come all this way to learn something of the mother he'd never known, so although her behaviour so far had been hardly welcoming, he had to overcome Dottie's suspicion and distrust somehow.

'Why did she call you Charles? Or did your father do that?'

The questions were so unexpected Charles swallowed some cocoa the wrong way and had to cough before he could answer.

'No, my mother named me—well, she and my father chose the names before I was born. Apparently, they both liked Charles as a name, then Edouard after my father's father and Albert after hers.'

He looked directly at Dottie.

'Your husband was called Albert, wasn't he?'

He thought the scowl she gave him might be all the answer he'd get, but then she said, 'Bertie—we called him Bertie!' in such a gruff tone Charles guessed at the emotion she was holding in check.

And why wouldn't there be emotion? How would he have felt if she'd suddenly turned up at home?

Overwhelmed, to say the least.

He set aside the rest of his toast and moved his chair a little closer to the bed.

'I know this must be a terrible shock for you, but I did write a couple of times and never received a reply so it seemed the only thing to do was to come. I'll go away again as soon as your flood goes down, if that's what you want.'

The scowl turned to a full-blown glare.

'I do *not* open letters with foreign stamps,' she said. 'You do not know what germs they might be carrying. It's how they spread anthrax, you know.'

Though slightly startled by the pronouncement, most of Charles's attention had turned to Jo, who had her eyes shut and her hand to her belly.

That, he *knew*, was a contraction!

Had his inattention drawn Dottie's eyes to Jo so that she said, 'If that was a contraction, look at your watch and start timing them.'

After which she lifted the table off her legs, set it aside on the bed, and clambered out, remarkably spry for someone who looked about a hundred.

'And don't worry,' she added, crossing the room to Jo. 'I've delivered most of the people still alive in the village, grandparents, parents and even some of the older children. I'll take care of you.'

The look of horror on Jo's face told Charles what she thought of that idea, but she rallied.

'That's very kind, Dottie, but I'm a doctor, I should be able to manage. I mean, don't women in some developing countries give birth in the fields where they are working, then wrap the baby in a sling on their back and keep working? If they can do that, I should be able to manage.'

She closed her eyes, pausing as another contraction tightened her belly.

'Anyway,' she added, 'I absolutely can*not* have the baby now. It's not Christmas Day, and Chris and Alice can't get through, and you know they want to be here.'

'You've got no choice, my girl,' Dottie told her. 'And too bad if they can't be here. I never did approve of them using you like this.'

Jo lifted her hand.

'Please, Dottie, no more of that. And I'll be glad of your help, but perhaps...'

She turned to Charles.

'You'd have a mobile, wouldn't you? If I do go properly into labour, we could start with video chat on my mobile and if it runs out of charge, could we use yours?'

'You want your labour going out on video chat?' Charles asked, totally bewildered by the speed at which things had moved from his meeting with his grandmother to possibly having to deliver a total stranger's baby in the midst of the gale that thrashed the windows and shook the house. 'With who, and why?'

'Only to Chris and Alice,' Jo said. 'You see, it's their baby.'

She spoke as if that explained everything, though from Charles's point of view it only made things more confusing.

Their baby?

'You're a surrogate?'

But even as he asked the question he watched the colour drain from Jo's face, and knew it was another contraction, a bad one. Childbirth hurt. So why would she go through it for someone else?

And how would she feel when it came time to hand over the baby she'd carried—nurtured—for nine months?

Now Dottie was issuing orders so he couldn't pursue the matter.

'Take the supper things down to the kitchen,' she was saying to him. 'Then when you get back I'll tell you where to find clean linen. There are some sheets that are washed so thin they're soft, and plenty of old towels. We'd better use this room, because the others all leak. The little chaise longue should be ideal because the back of it only comes halfway. And gloves, I suppose. There might be gloves in the kitchen!'

'Washing-up gloves?' Jo said faintly. 'You're going to deliver Lulu with washing-up gloves?'

'You just relax,' Dottie ordered. 'We'll do whatever is necessary.'

Charles carried the half-eaten meal down to the kitchen, wondering whether he should get out of this madness before he caught whatever brought it on!

Was the road really flooded?

And *that* thought horrified him!

Surely he wasn't thinking of leaving these women on their own—one to deliver her baby, the other as dotty as her name.

Of course he couldn't, flooded road or not.

So he carried his burden to the kitchen, noticed the bucket was full on the way and came back to empty it, checking there was no new stranger standing at the door before he threw the water.

Back upstairs for more orders! That part at least was a novelty. At home, and at the hospital, he was more likely to be giving them...

Jo closed her eyes and wondered if she willed it hard enough she could stop the contractions.

Forget about it!

But what about Chris and Alice? her mind protested.

Charge your mobile.

She stood up, ignored Dottie's shriek that she

needed to wait for the next contraction to time it, and went to her bedroom, where, by some miracle, her mobile was already on the charger and, even more wonderful, fully charged.

The linen cupboard was her next destination. He might be willing, this Charles who'd appeared from nowhere, but she doubted he'd fathom the system in Dottie's linen cupboard.

But Dottie had been right, there were sheets washed to a softness that could be used to clean and wrap a newborn, and plenty of old towels—Dottie rarely parted with anything—on which the baby could be delivered. And she could cut up some of the old sheets to use as nappies—they'd be softer than the towels...

She pulled out an armful of each, then, because it felt good to be standing, she walked along the hall, avoiding buckets on the way, then back again.

Walking was good, until the next contraction came—far too close to the previous one—and she leant against the wall, the linen pillowed in her arms.

'Was that a contraction?' Dottie asked, peering out the bedroom door to see where her patient had gone.

Jo nodded, so bemused to discover she was thinking of herself as Dottie's patient she couldn't manage words.

The pain passed and she carried the linen through to Dottie's room, then turned back. What she really needed was a shower—and just in case this baby really was coming, she'd have a shower, put on a clean nightdress and—

And what?

No! The baby couldn't come. She wasn't ready! Chris and Alice weren't ready! And worst of all, there was this stupid low off the coast with wind gusts too strong for a helicopter to make it out here if anything went wrong—not with her so much, but with the baby...

She considered crying, so great was the frustration, but she wasn't the crying type—tall, well-built women couldn't get away with tears the way petite women could. Besides which, she'd never seen the point. What good did it do? *And* it made her eyes red! She'd have a shower. That way, if she did happen to cry—well, in the shower, who could tell...?

She stood under the streaming hot water for so long it began to turn cold. She knew the ancient hot-water system would take hours to heat it again and felt guilty about using it all, though Charles and Dottie had already showered.

The next contraction was strong enough for her to grab the washbasin to hold herself steady until it passed.

This *couldn't* be happening!

It was bad enough that she'd spent the last weeks of this pregnancy wondering how she could stop herself shrieking or swearing in front of Chris and Alice, but in front of Dottie and the stranger?

Dear Heaven! What *was* she to do? Didn't soldiers in bygone times bite on bullets while surgeons extracted other bullets from their wounds.

How did they not break their teeth? she wondered as she walked back to her room.

Not that Dottie would have a bullet to bite on— at least Jo hoped not, although with Dottie you couldn't be sure of anything.

Another wave of pain washed over her. This was ridiculous, she thought as she gripped the end of the bed for support. Baby was two weeks early when the obstetrician had assured her it would be late, and she was out on the bluff with the worst weather in a hundred years raging all around her, and a total stranger and an eighty-five-year-old midwife for support!

Not that she doubted Dottie's ability to do anything she set her mind to—sheer stubbornness would see to that!

As the pain ebbed, Jo pulled out a clean nightshirt, packed because it was slightly more decent than the long T-shirts she usually wore to bed, and she'd thought she might have to get up to Dottie in the night. She put cream on her face and sat on the bed, her hands on the low swell of her belly.

And images she didn't want came flooding back, sitting like this on a hospital bed at fifteen years old, a child still herself, about to have a child—a child she was going to give away.

Then Gran had been there, in her head, Gran's arms around her shoulders, telling her it would all be all right and to think how happy someone would be—the couple waiting for the baby, as Chris and Alice were waiting for this one.

And everything *had* been all right.

Another contraction brought her back to the here and now—with a vengeance! She rode the wave of pain, checked her watch, and realised she'd have to leave the sanctuary of her room.

At least if she had the baby here and now she'd be spared the indignity of a hospital gown that invariably left the wearer's backside hanging out. Should she phone Chris and Alice now, or wait until she was certain this was going to be the main event?

Unable to decide, she emptied the upstairs buckets again, then paced the corridor, up and back and up and back, not wanting to return to Dottie's room with nothing more than a purple and white striped nightshirt covering her body.

Charles appeared at some stage of her pacing, fitting his step to hers.

'I know it probably helps to keep moving but at some stage I need to check on your cervix to see how dilated it is.'

A complete stranger checking out *her* cervix?

Particularly this handsome and apparently princely stranger...

Panic welled inside her and for all she told herself that most of the doctors she saw were strangers at first, nothing eased the disturbing thought of this man looking at her most private parts.

'Dottie can do that,' she said, and the man had the hide to smile.

'I have no doubt at all about that,' he said. 'I rather imagine she can do anything she sets her mind to, but she is frail, and a little arthritic, I imagine. It would be easier for me to check.'

And as another wave of pain was clutching at Jo's body she couldn't argue. In fact, it was bad enough, she realised as it waned, that she wasn't really going to care who did what to her as long as they got Lulu safely out.

And soon!

'Do you have to do it now?' she muttered ungraciously at him.

'I think so,' he said, putting an arm around her waist to steady her as she straightened up from the wall. 'It will give us some idea of how far along you are, and if Dottie has happened to keep an old stethoscope, I should be able to hear the baby's heartbeats as well, to check it's all right.'

'*Her* heartbeats—*she's* all right!' Jo reminded him, but all he did was smile and continue to guide her towards Dottie's room with his arm around her waist.

Totally unnecessary—at least until she stiffened as her belly tightened and another wave of pain rose inside her. She clung to him, and felt the strength in the arms that held her. Wondering how a prince might get strong arms diverted her momentarily, until keeping back the urge to yell blocked everything but the pain from her mind.

Dottie had covered the end of the low chaise longue with clean towels and was now engaged in tearing the fine old sheets into large squares.

'We can dry it with some of these then swaddle it. We'll think about nappies and such later.'

She must have caught sight of Jo's pale face.

'Coming faster, are they?' she said. 'Well, get up there so we can check your cervix. If it's not already dilated to seven or eight centimetres, you might as well go to bed in your room and try to get some sleep. It will be a long night.'

Jo, who'd managed between pains to subside onto the chaise, tried to work out Dottie's thinking. She rarely did any obstetrics work herself but *was* aware that the cervix started thinning out and dilating over the days and sometimes weeks before the active phase of labour began.

'I imagine she's been timing your contractions better than you have,' Charles said, answering her unspoken question. 'You're well into the active phase of labour, hence her guess.'

'But we'll have to get the phones ready. Mine's fully charged in my room across the passage. Would you use yours too? Please?'

'Will you stop whispering and concentrate on what you're here to do,' Dottie said in an exasperated voice, as she threw a light sheet over Jo's lower body and levered her legs up to they were bent at the knees. 'I'm quite capable of holding a phone if someone gets the number and sets the camera on go. If this bloke is a doctor, then we'll let him do the business. You're pretty low down and I don't bend as well as I once did.'

But the words were lost in a haze of pain, while Jo gripped the high side of the makeshift bed and gritted her teeth so tightly she wondered if she'd break them.

Even without the bullet, she thought grimly as the wave diminished.

'Close to ten,' she heard Charles say, but the wave returned with renewed ferocity, and she heard herself yell to someone, anyone, to get her phone.

'Chris and Alice, under C in the friends list,'

she panted, now imagining Lulu's passage down the birth canal. Sliding forward with the contraction, retreating slightly as it passed.

And Chris and Alice not here to experience it…

Tears formed in her eyes and she tasted blood as she bit down on her lower lip.

'You're allowed to yell, or moan, or even swear, you know,' Charles said, squatting at the bottom of the chaise with her phone focused on her dilated cervix.

So moan she did as the next contraction seized her tortured body, although through the haze of pain she heard Charles order Dottie to take over filming, telling them the head had crowned.

Did she push now? She tried to remember her classes. No, maybe not now—let Lulu come out gently. But hadn't she pushed earlier? Pushed, puffed, panted—she'd been relying on Chris and Alice who'd attended all the antenatal classes with her to tell her what to do when, but now she was too tired to remember any of it, while her first experience had been wiped completely from her memory!

And now the contractions had stopped—well, eased at least—and Charles and Dottie were whispering at the bottom of the bed.

'What's happened?' Jo demanded, as a cold sense of dread enveloped her exhausted body.

'There, all's well,' she heard Charles say, as the small, wet mortal in his hands finally let out a cry.

'Not a Lulu, I'm afraid,' he said, coming close to reef open the buttons on Jo's nightshirt and place the baby on her chest, his head towards her breasts. 'Let's see how his instinct is.'

He was beaming down at Jo, while Dottie had come around to the side of the bed, still filming—ignoring the conversations being flung at her from the other end of the phone.

'See,' Charles said, while Jo watched in amazement as the tiny newborn wiggled his way across her body to latch onto a nipple. 'He's fine—he'll do. We've no drugs to help expel the placenta but if you let him suckle, and I massage you a bit, that should work.'

Dottie, having abandoned the phone now the main event was over, draped a soft sheet across the two of them, then glared at Charles across the bed.

'My way would have worked just as well,' she said, so much belligerence in her tone, Jo was frowning as she looked at them.

'What way? What are you talking about?' she asked when it became apparent no one was going to enlighten her.

'He was born flat,' Charles explained, 'but I cleared the mucus from his mouth and blew a breath into him and you heard his squawk.'

'In my day,' Dottie said, drawing herself up to her full five feet one and glaring at Charles across the bed, 'we flicked the sole of the foot with a finger and that made them cry—worked every time.'

Jo smiled, then looked down at the little bundle in her arms.

Letting him suckle was good.

They'd agreed, she, Alice and Chris, that the baby should take advantage of the colostrum in her breasts to help ward off infection. Had it all gone to plan, she'd have taken tablets to stop her milk coming in but the early arrival and the state of the floods had put paid to that.

She might have to feed him for a day or two, but that was okay. Right from the day she'd taken the decision to act as a surrogate she'd realised she had to stay focused on the pregnancy as a job, something she was undertaking for someone else, so although her hormones had gone all weird on her, she'd always been totally aware that this baby wasn't hers, and feeding him wouldn't change that.

Although she'd hardly have been human if she didn't feel a thrill to hold the little fellow to her breast, and she smiled up at Charles, thanking him, pleased he'd been here to help her through it all, calm and efficient—a perfect prince of a man, in fact!

She smiled again at the silly thought and, looking up, caught him smiling back, a look of such pride on his face she knew the miracle of birth had affected him as well.

Charles looked down at the mother and child, full of a feeling of pride that he'd pulled off a successful delivery, mixed with a kind of wondrous pleasure about the miracle of birth.

He saw serenity under the tiredness in Jo's face, but something else that puzzled him.

Distance?

A lack of pride?

Some kind of pain?

Because the baby wasn't hers?

Or because of something that had happened in the past?

The dread thought of rape crossed his mind, but he knew that women didn't have to proceed with an unwanted pregnancy these days.

He studied Jo again—yes, she was tired, but... detached too. That was the word he sought.

Was it not affecting her at all?

Or was she fighting whatever her hormones were telling her to stay detached from this child she had to give away?

But why were *his* emotions in such an uproar?

Was it being here in his mother's house that had made him susceptible to this sudden attraction?

Probably!

He looked around the room. Dottie had disappeared, and the phone she'd been using was ringing.

'Could you answer that?' Jo asked, gesturing to where it lay on a side table. 'It will be Chris and Alice—they'll want to see him.'

He had picked up the phone when Dottie returned to the room with a basin of water—warm, he hoped—more towels, and a hefty pair of scissors dangling from one finger.

'You're way ahead of me,' he told her, as he lifted the phone and pressed the button to answer it.

'Can we see her?'

Two excited voices rumbled in his ear and he switched the phone back to video chat mode and held it out to show the baby lying on Jo's chest.

Jo gestured for the phone.

'He's fine, although he's not a Lulu but a Louis. I'm fine, we'll see you as soon as the water goes down, but right now there's stuff we have to do, and we all need a sleep.'

She shut down the phone.

'We'll have to turn it off, they'll be ringing every ten minutes.'

'Damn silly idea, I said so all along,' Dottie was muttering as she carefully lifted the baby boy and set him on the bed to dry him off.

'Take these,' she said to Charles, producing two large stainless-steel pegs from a pocket of her Chinese robe. 'I've poured bleach over them so they should be sterile.'

Charles thought back to training days and knew exactly what was required. He clamped the cord at both ends then cut between the clamps. And with a quick twist of his fingers, the cord on the baby's end was tied, a little nub still sticking out, to dry, and fall off later.

There, baby boy, he thought as he worked, you'll have something to remember me for ever, your neat little belly button.

And as Dottie wasn't watching, he touched the baby's cheek, smiling when he opened huge eyes to check out who was near him. And the lump in his throat was probably from tiredness.

Jo had turned on her side to watch Dottie ministering to the baby, and although he guessed she'd have been happy doing that herself, she didn't want to take the fun away from her old friend.

Once satisfied he was dry and comfortable, Dottie swaddled him in a square of sheet, and handed him back to Jo.

'Try to keep him suckling, it will help with this last stage,' she said firmly, although Charles fancied he could see the glassiness of tears in her eyes.

She was as affected as he was by the birth…

By the time the placenta was delivered, Jo had drifted off to sleep, and as he helped Dottie clean up he realised that the wind had lessened and the rain no longer thundered down on the damaged roof.

'It'll be gone by tomorrow,' Dottie told him, peering out the window, a bundle of towels in her arms.

'And the road to the village?'

'It'll go down at low tide. Might flood a little more when the tide comes in again but not enough to cut us off.'

'And Jo and the baby?'

He *had* to ask.

Would the parents just turn up and take the infant?

How would Jo feel about that?

Surely it had to affect her—she'd carried the baby for nine months after all.

'Hmph!' Dottie said. 'Damn fool idea right from the start. Would you believe they'd phone poor Jo at all hours of the day and night and she'd have to put the phone on her belly while they talked to Lulu. And they sent music she had to play to her. As if a developing foetus would hear all that going on, let alone understand it.'

'They took the surrogacy thing that far?'

Charles asked, wondering just how much of a trial this pregnancy must have been for Jo.

'Oh, she's told you, has she? Dottie said. 'Come down to the laundry while I get rid of this lot and I'll explain,' Dottie told him, and, sensing a slight weakening towards him on the part of his grandmother, Charles was only too willing to go along.

'Alice couldn't carry children and they longed for a baby of their own, so Jo offered to be a surrogate. Stupid idea! Worse timing! She had a perfectly good man who wanted to marry her then suddenly she's off having someone else's baby— well, he couldn't hang around nine months, could he?'

She paused, then, apparently needing to be honest, she added, 'Not that Jo was all that keen on him. Not keen on marriage at all. I think her home life as a child put her off.'

The slight tightness in his chest as he heard Dottie's words Charles put down to tiredness. It had been a long night and he hadn't finished his grilled cheese on toast before he'd been drawn into the drama of the birth.

Down in the antiquated laundry, Dottie was running cold water into a deep stone tub.

'We'll soak all this for now,' Dottie told him, although she was doing all the work. 'Then get Jo off to her own bed for the night, not that she'll get much sleep if the baby wakes through the night, which, of course, it will. That Chris and Alice are in for some fun!'

She pushed the towels and sheet into the cold water, pressing them down so they were all covered, then headed for a door he hadn't noticed before. The place was like a rabbit warren.

'Box room,' she said, throwing open the door. 'See if you can find a decent, dry box we can pack with sheets for the baby. Having got this far, it would kill Jo if she rolled on the little fellow in the night and smothered him.'

Charles had to smile as he peered into the unlit room. It was obvious cardboard boxes had been going there to die for years, possibly decades. Which made the ones at the top of the pile the newest and most likely to be sanitary.

Pleased to have been co-opted by Dottie to help—surely it would thaw her attitude towards him, if only a smidgen—he examined the boxes with care, finally producing a clean-looking one with KURL printed in blue along the top.

He had no idea what KURL might be—tinned food, paper, linen?—but he pulled it out and held it for Dottie to inspect.

'You'll have to cut down the sides,' Dottie told him, after a nod he took for approval. 'It wouldn't do for him to suffocate at this stage.'

She turned and led him from the room, through

the kitchen where he looked a little longingly at the debris of his supper.

'The scissors are in still in my bedroom, so we'll take it up there.'

And if he manoeuvred himself into a good position he might be able to see the photos on the chest of drawers.

Clutching his box like a prize, he waited until Dottie had ascended in her lift, then followed her up to find Jo awake, sitting on the little chaise, holding the baby in her arms and looking slightly bemused.

She smiled as he and Dottie came into the room.

'I obviously didn't dream it because there's this baby here to prove it, but I can hardly believe it all happened.'

'You'll believe it soon enough when he wakes you every couple of hours during the night,' Dottie told her, going forward to lift the infant from Jo's arms. 'Now, you go to bed and try to get some sleep. We'll fix a bed for him and put him by you.'

But Charles and his box had stopped in the doorway, transfixed by the sight of this woman, her red-gold hair wild and dishevelled around her pale face, the baby resting in her arms. It was a scene worthy of the great Pre-Raphaelite paintings, and he could only stare.

She's not keen on marriage.

'Well, are you going to cut the box?'

He hoped he hadn't been standing there more than a few seconds, for all it had seemed like a lifetime. He strode forward, smiling at Jo as he passed, taking the scissors from Dottie and hacking away at the sides of the makeshift crib.

'You do that and sort through the linen for padding. You need to keep it firm. I'll take Jo to her room,' Dottie ordered, still holding the baby and occasionally smiling down at him when she thought no one was watching.

Not as tough as she made out, this grandmother of his, Charles thought, but still a very redoubtable lady.

He'd kind of accidentally moved to the far side of the bed so as he cut the cardboard he could also take in the photos.

But although he'd hoped to see at least one of a young woman, or even a girl, who might be his mother, he was disappointed. There was Dottie as a young woman, in her nurse's white uniform, clutching a rolled certificate, and a handsome young man in army uniform he assumed would be his grandfather. Unfortunately, the wide-brimmed, slouch hat of the Australian Army shadowed the man's face and before he could do more than glance at the rest he heard Dottie returning.

Hastily dropping the cut pieces on the floor, he put the scissors on the bedside table, grabbed a sheet and wadded it into the bottom of the box, then put a cut sheet, wide enough to swaddle the baby, over it.

'That should do,' Dottie told him, although she seemed reluctant to relinquish the baby into his new bed.

'You'd better get some sleep yourself,' she said instead, as Charles picked up the debris from the floor and stood there wondering what on earth to do next. 'If you turn left at the top of the stairs you'll come to the front room, though why it's always called that I don't know. But it has a view if ever it stops raining—looks south and west towards Anooka.'

He had to say *something*, Charles knew, but what?

He went with courtesy.

'Thank you,' he said. 'It's very good of you to take me in. I hadn't realised just how isolated this place would be. I had arranged accommodation— well, the hospital at Anooka had arranged it—but having come all this way I wanted—'

'Why should the hospital have arranged accommodation for you?' Dottie demanded, definitely frosty now.

Charles shrugged. It seemed silly now, given Dottie's reaction to his arrival, but the old cliché

about a person might as well being hung for a
sheep as a lamb seemed appropriate here so he
told her.

'I thought, when I decided to come to see you,
that it wouldn't be fair to either of us if I just
came for a few days. I wanted to learn something of what my mother's life would have been
like growing up here, so I came in on a six-week
working visa, sponsored by the Anooka and District Hospital Board. Apparently, they are only
too happy to have British-trained doctors to fill
in as locums, especially over Christmas.'

'You're here for six weeks?' Dottie demanded,
finally placing the baby in his new bed.

'It seemed only right,' Charles said, aware it
sounded a little weak.

'And you got the hospital to arrange your accommodation?'

The demand was shriller this time, as if the diminutive woman was getting more and more annoyed, though why remained a mystery.

'Did you think my home might not be good
enough for you?'

Her voice cracked and he realised that she must
be exhausted.

He could hardly mention the unanswered letters
again, so he said, very gently, 'I thought it might
be inconvenient for you, but right now we've both
got a bed to go to, so maybe we should both get

some sleep. I'll take the baby in to Jo's room, shall I? I'll go in quietly so she doesn't wake up. It's across the passage, isn't it, her room?'

Dottie nodded, but it was a tired nod, so Charles lifted little KURL in his box and quietly departed, pausing at the door to say, 'Sleep well!'

Would she?

He doubted it.

A grandson blown in by the storm, and a baby delivered the same night. It was a hell of a lot for an elderly woman to take in.

He pushed opened the door of Jo's bedroom, narrowly avoiding a bucket just inside it, and, checking there were no more leaks, he laid the box beside the bed, pleased the stormclouds still overhead were blotting out the stars and moon, because seeing Jo sleeping by moonlight might have been more than he could handle.

Downstairs, he found his bag, had another quick and barely lukewarm shower in the servants' quarters—at least he hadn't been banished to sleep down here—and made his way up to the room Dottie had indicated.

The three buckets with their musically tinkling drips told him his original assumption was right—this room undoubtedly had the worst leaks.

He checked the buckets—half-full, two of them. So he tipped the smallest amount into one of the others and took the two to the bathroom down the passage. He emptied them into the bath then realised he should have checked Jo's bucket.

He went back into her bedroom, but as he quietly pushed open the door he saw the bedside light was on and she was sitting up in bed, the baby at her breast.

He didn't believe in love at first sight, but of course this wasn't first sight. He'd had more to do with this woman—learned more of her—in the last twenty-four hours than most people would do in six months. And seeing her there, her vividly beautiful hair tumbling onto her shoulders, he knew what he felt was more than just attraction. It was deeper, clearer somehow—something the attraction part was clouding because it was so strong.

Or maybe he was just plain exhausted! It had been a *very* long day...

'Bucket,' he mumbled, grabbing it and backing out the door. Cursing himself for his idiotic behaviour, he emptied it, returned it, mumbled an almost inarticulate 'Goodnight' and departed, back to his own rather watery room, strung so tight there was no way he'd sleep.

CHAPTER THREE

EXCEPT HE DID, waking with sun streaming through his windows, and sounds of great joy echoing up from downstairs. He was halfway to the door, intending to lean over the bannister to see what was happening, when he realised he was naked, another hangover from student days.

He grabbed the coverlet and wrapped it around his waist, then went out quietly.

Not that he needed to be quiet, so loud was the excitement.

A couple, apparently Alice and Chris, were standing close together, both peering down at a small, tightly wrapped bundle in Alice's arms, and crowing loudly about his beauty, and his likeness to one or both of them.

Jo stood behind them, smiling broadly, while from her perch on the stair lift at the bottom of the stairs, Dottie watched the proceedings with dour disapproval.

Not one to get too excited about things, his grandmother!

He backed away into his room to dress, used the upstairs bathroom to wash and shave, then, as the noise from the bottom of the stairs showed no sign of abating, decided he'd go down, make all the right noises and disappear into the kitchen, where at least he knew how to work the toaster.

But life was never that easy. He had to be thanked, his hand pumped, his cheek kissed, the baby offered for inspection.

Jo, perhaps catching sight of his discomfort, said, 'Alice and Chris brought us supplies. They're in the kitchen.'

It was the only prompt he needed, and as Dottie leapt off her perch at these magic words, he followed her into the kitchen.

'You got children?' she asked, as she rummaged through the carrier bags piled on the kitchen table, finally coming out with a box of a dozen eggs.

'No, I'm not married,' he told her.

She looked up at him with a 'Hmph!' before adding, 'That doesn't seem to mean much these days, though I suppose being a prince it'd be a bit different. Not but what those English princes in the olden days had dozens of illegitimate children!'

As there seemed no reasonable reply to this, he asked if she'd like toast.

'Yes, but only with my eggs,' she told him. 'I like two, soft boiled, just two minutes from the time the water bubbles, mind. You'll find the egg-cups in the cupboard under the toaster and the pots in the cupboard by the stove.'

Charles hid a smile. Had she once had servants at her beck and call, or had Jo been looking after her so well she'd come to expect being waited on?

Not that he minded in the least. The more time he spent with her, the more chance he had of her finally talking to him about his mother.

Jo, entering the kitchen a few minutes later, was surprised to find the table had been cleared of groceries, and from the way Dottie was sitting in her usual place with her placemat in front of her and the good china awaiting toast and tea, she'd quickly trained the visitor.

He was rescuing eggs from a pot, and pre-sented them to Dottie, one in the pretty eggcup she always used, the other lying on the plate by its side.

'You should hit the end with a spoon so they stop cooking,' Dottie told him, quite kindly, Jo thought. 'It stops them going hard in their shell.'

She had tapped both eggs as she spoke, then, noticing Jo, she said, 'Would you like eggs, Jo?'

Charles's smile told Jo he knew exactly what the older woman was doing, but she shook her head.

'The box baby and I had breakfast at about five this morning, thank you. I told Chris and Alice I'd say goodbye for them. According to the local weather reports, we could be cut off again at high tide and they wanted to get the baby home. They've been ready for his arrival for months— for all they were sure it was a her and would arrive on Christmas Day. But they do have plentiful supplies of nappies and formula, which is all a baby really needs at this stage.'

She paused, checking her own reactions to the handover, and found she really wasn't upset. Though probably that was a lot to do with having been up with him every hour during the night. But she was pleased to find that she didn't mind—that her detachment right from the start had stood her in good stead.

And having sorted all that out in her head, she remembered her manners.

'I've got to thank you both so much for all you did last night. I'd never have managed on my own.'

'You did most of the work,' Dottie reminded her, as she lifted a spoonful of egg to her lips and tasted it, nodding in approval.

'And well done to you, young man. That's a

very good egg, though I suppose once you start work you'll be living closer to the hospital so you won't be doing my eggs in the morning.'

'I could do them on my days off, if you'll have me here,' Charles replied, not turning from where he was making more toast, presumably for himself.

Start work?

Days off?

What?

Jo looked across at him and then at Dottie. What had she missed?

'Of course you'll come here,' Dottie was saying, which was even more surprising.

Although she'd offered Jo accommodation while the locum was living in Jo's house, Dottie would soon tire of company. She liked her solitude as much as Jo did—and she'd send both of them on their way.

But she was obviously beginning to accept this man as her grandson if she'd insisted he could stay on his time off!

It was too much for Jo's tired mind to sort out…

She found out about the work thing a little later. Charles had been set the task of emptying all the buckets and returning them to a cupboard in the laundry. Jo had protested that she could do it, but Dottie had been adamant.

'You need to rest,' she told Jo, 'and don't give me any of that fiddle-faddle about women working in the fields. Just slow down a bit, get your strength back. The Prince tells me he's come here to work for a while, so he might as well stay here until he's due to start instead of paying rent in some ratty hospital flat.'

Left speechless by this turnaround in Dottie's attitude to Charles, she sneaked after him into the laundry where he was trying, without much luck, to fit all twelve buckets into the cupboard.

'You put some of them in the box room,' Jo said. 'That's where I found the extra ones.'

He turned to her and smiled.

'Do you think the fact that she's giving me orders means she's accepted me as a relative?' he asked, and Jo, who was trying to ignore the way the smile had made her feel—hormone imbalance for sure—shook her head.

'I think it's more likely that she's finding a malicious pleasure in giving orders to a prince—or to someone who *might* be a prince.'

He smiled again and she had to hope that her leftover pregnancy hormones settled down quickly before she made a fool of herself over this man. She'd just had a baby, for heaven's sake, and even though it wasn't her baby, surely she shouldn't be feeling this way.

Although maybe the baby had more to do with it than she'd realised. It *had* felt good to hold the little mortal in her arms—felt *right* somehow—as if the shadows of the past had been wiped away…

Though that didn't amount to a hill of beans as far as feeling attraction to the Prince was concerned.

'He's a *prince*, for heaven's sake, so stop reacting to a smile,' she muttered to herself as she escaped, deciding to do as Dottie said and go to her room.

Not to rest, but to calm down and attempt to find her normal, practical self, or, failing that, discover something else to occupy her mind so completely that she'd barely notice the man was there.

Or have time to think about babies!

And how likely was either of those scenarios? Big sigh!

She could have gone home, only the locum was staying there and she didn't want to intrude or make him feel uncomfortable. Could she put him off? Find another locum position for him and go back to work herself?

Hardly fair on him when he was supposed to be there another four weeks!

So, the only thing to do was keep busy, and she already knew there was plenty to keep her busy in Dottie's house.

So, as the low moved south in the following days, taking the howling winds and torrential rain with it, Jo moved through the old house like a whirl-wind, flinging open windows to let in the sun-shine, mopping up the damp floors, dusting, polishing, ordering more food to be delivered, and cooking spectacular meals.

'That's more like my Jo,' Dottie, who had taken to following Charles around the house, said to him one day. He was balancing on a rather rickety ladder—circa 1924, he rather thought—taking down curtains Jo wished to wash. 'She's always hated being idle, and while that locum she found is still there, she can't go back to work.'

Charles took this in, although more of his mind was on *his* continued presence in the house. He'd been in touch with the hospital and knew they had a job for him from next week.

But to stay here until then?

Was Dottie serious about that?

Or was she letting him stay because Jo, in her burst of frenetic activity, usually inveigled him into helping her, although most of the things he did she'd have managed on her own.

And Dottie *had* intimated that she expected him to stay…

But these days were a mixed blessing as far as he was concerned. Part of it was to do with seeing so much of Jo, getting to know more of the way she moved, and thought, and smiled—and becoming increasingly aware of the attraction he felt towards her.

On the other hand, being in the house where his mother had grown up, seeing it polished and shining as it must have been when she'd lived in it, he longed to imagine her there—to picture her in the sunny living room, the old-fashioned kitchen, the windswept garden with the thick succulent plants with huge pink flowers that apparently enjoyed blasts of salt air.

He knew coming here had probably been a mad impulse, but although he knew the time had come to marry and have children—as was his duty—something had tugged at him from the far side of the world, some need to know more about the woman who'd given birth to him, about her life, and her place in this family.

But how could he find the right image of his mother, when Dottie remained tight-lipped about her daughter?

Although he *was* learning more about this side of his family, and that, too, was important to him.

He knew his grandfather had fought the Japanese in New Guinea at the end of the Second World War and returned a hero—at least in the eyes of the locals. He'd gone on to become Mayor of Anooka, and, apparently, there was a statue of him near the town hall.

Charles knew he'd see it eventually, but statues couldn't talk.

'Dottie adored him,' Jo said to him one day, when they were in the kitchen three days after the dramatic birth, cleaning decades of baked-on food out of the old oven. 'My grandmother, who was one of Dottie's best friends, was always a bit amused by her devotion. He was older, you see, Dottie's Bertie—well, your grandfather I guess— and my Gran always said that made him easier to worship.'

Charles tucked this new titbit of his history away as Jo continued, 'And he *was* a lovely man, Gran said—kind and thoughtful and generous— but he was still a man and as far as Gran was concerned, that made him an inferior species.'

'Yet she married one,' Charles pointed out, 'or you wouldn't be here.'

Jo took her head out of the oven for long enough to smile at him.

'Purely to procreate, she maintained.'

She paused for a moment before adding, 'And that might actually be true, for she divorced him not long after her third child—my mother—was born.'

Charles, who was struggling with an urge to wipe a smudge of grease off Jo's upper lip, smiled, then bumped his head on the table as he tried to stand, brought back to earth by Dottie's sudden appearance in the kitchen.

'Shouldn't you be doing that, instead of Jo?' Dottie said to him. 'She's just had a baby.'

Charles grinned at his grandmother.

'I *have* offered,' he said, 'and she doesn't think I'll do it right, so all I'm allowed to do is rinse out the cleaning cloths and refill the sudsy bucket from time to time.

'Besides,' he added, 'I rather think it's something to do with women working in the fields, pausing to give birth and strap the baby on their back—or maybe it was front—and get on with their jobs. I think she wants to prove she's the equal of any farmhand.'

'Damn silly nonsense, but then the whole thing has been just that!'

And Dottie stumped out of the room.

'What happened to Bertie?' Charles asked, when he heard the stair lift ascending and knew it was safe to talk.

But Jo, who usually answered all his questions about Dottie, remained silent, scrubbing away at an apparently extra-dirty spot.

Or avoiding the question?

Intrigued, Charles persisted.

Well, it was that, or imagining just how soft Jo's flesh might feel if he accidentally bumped against it. It was soft and pale, and he knew her skin would feel like silk if he ran his fingers over it.

Forget Jo!

'Did he die young?'

More silence, but that now Charles considered it, he'd seen photos of his grandfather in his mayoral robes and chain of office and he hadn't seemed all that young.

Seventyish, perhaps.

'You don't know?'

As if taking this last question as a slight on her family knowledge, Jo emerged from the oven, squatted back on her heels and stared at him.

Studying him for some reason?

Deciding whether he deserved an answer?

Or perhaps needed one...

She couldn't just keep staring at him, Jo thought to herself—not that he wasn't worth the odd stare—but seeing that darkly attractive face, those dark, dark eyes, and lips that were made for seduction—hormones still rioting—didn't provide an answer.

'It's really Dottie's place to tell you what you need to know,' she finally said.

'Except she won't,' Charles reminded her. 'She won't talk about anything personal. What's more, unless I'm very much mistaken, some of the few photos in the living room have disappeared. I'm sure there was one of a man in some kind of fancy uniform, and it's gone now.'

Jo sighed. Charles had come a long way to find his family; to learn something of the mother he never knew. And if Dottie wouldn't tell...

'He had a stroke.'

There, that bit was out. Maybe she needn't mention when, although she wasn't one hundred percent certain about the when, just had a vague feeling there was a connection.

'How long ago? How old was he? Did he die immediately or get over it or was he badly damaged by it? "He had a stroke" can't be the end of the story.'

Jo knew her lips had closed into a mutinous line, but she resisted the urge to shove her head back into the oven—and possibly clamber in after it.

'Bad,' she said. 'Bad enough that he was flown to Sydney and kept there for nearly a year—operations, rehab, OT and speech therapy—everything Dottie could think of to help him regain just a smidgen of independence. According to Gran, she was determined he'd get over it, and when nothing worked, she brought him home.'

'Hence the stair lift she really doesn't need?'

'Oh, she loves that. I think it gives her a thrill—hence the speed at which she travels—but Bertie...'

Jo paused.

'She pretended, Gran said, that he was fine. She washed and dressed him every morning, brought him downstairs and fed him breakfast, took him for a walk along the clifftop in his wheelchair, talking to him all the time, convinced he knew exactly where he was and what she was saying.'

Jo saw in Charles's eyes that he was realising just how immense this task must have been—how time-consuming—*and* how much it spoke of love.

She returned to her task, hoping she'd given him enough to think about for a while, so he'd stop asking questions.

But, really, the oven was as clean as she was going to get it, and she couldn't keep her head stuck in there for ever.

She gave the sides a final swipe with the cloth, backed out and stood up to replace the shelves she'd already cleaned—well, Charles had cleaned.

Lifting up the bucket, she chuckled as he pretended to flinch away from her, and went through to the laundry to clean up.

What a mess, she thought as she scrubbed grease from her arms. At least she'd known her mother—known, and loved, and been loved by her for fourteen years. And for all *her* upbringing had been unconventional, to say the least, the people at the commune had been an extended family.

Too close a family in the end…

But then she'd had Gran. She'd found an address in an old book of her mother's and she'd run away to find her—totally bewildered by what was happening in her body, aware women became pregnant but not believing it could possibly have happened to her.

Through Gran, she had come to know her real relations—at least, the ones that Gran spoke to…

But as she returned to the kitchen where Charles was setting out tea things on a silver tray—under Dottie's supervision—she realised she should have been thinking of ways to overcome this silly attraction she was feeling towards the visitor, not worrying about families—either his or hers.

'We're taking tea in the garden,' Dottie announced. 'If you could wait for the kettle to boil and make the tea then bring it out, Charles can organise chairs for us all.'

Charles winked at Jo over the tray before turning to follow Dottie out, for all the world like a butler following the mistress of the house.

Was it just for the sheer delight of having a prince cook her breakfast and fetch and carry for her that Dottie was treating Charles like this, or was it some kind of test she was setting him?

For the hundredth time, Jo wished she'd known Dottie's daughter. Had she been dutiful and obedient right up until the day she'd gone off with the vagabond, or had she always refused to fall into line with Dottie's wishes?

In which case, Dottie could be getting her own back through the son.

Jo shook her head. That simply didn't feel right.

She knew Dottie as a kind and generous friend. Irascible at times, certainly, and not one to suffer fools gladly, but at heart she was a good woman.

The kettle boiled and Jo made the tea, knowing by now exactly how Dottie liked it. She put the silver pot on the tray already holding a small jug of milk and a sugar bowl, and carried it out to the garden.

Obviously acting on instructions, Charles had set up the small outdoor table and chairs under the huge poinciana tree, denuded of many of its fronds of fine leaves, but still offering enough shelter from the hot December sun.

Jo set down her tray and looked around. She had a patient who did some gardening for Dottie;

he wouldn't mind coming in to clean up the debris of the storm. But it was sight of the sea that disturbed Jo more than the wind-ravaged garden.

'Something wrong?' Charles asked, and she realised she must be frowning.

'It's the swell,' she said, moving back towards the table where Dottie was pouring tea. 'It'll stay up for days and it means the waves will be huge and probably choppy.'

'And they'll have to cancel the surf carnival,' Dottie announced in such delight Charles could only stare at her.

'You don't like surf carnivals? I thought they'd become part of the Australian culture. Don't some of the world's best surfers come from Australia?'

'Hmph!' from Dottie, so it was left to Jo to explain.

'The Port Anooka Carnival is one of the oldest on the east coast. It's not the biggest and it's no longer on the world surfing circuit, but it retains the old carnival atmosphere. People who've been surfing all their lives—some of them now in their eighties—turn up in their campervans and old cars and strive to relive the days when it all began.'

'Damn fool idea!' Dottie muttered. 'Place gets overrun by ageing hippies for days. Fair rides on the esplanade, and kids running wild through the village.'

'Well, I was sixteen the first time I came here on holiday with Gran, and I thought the whole thing was magical. You could sit on the cliff above North Beach and watch the surfing all day, then go to the fair at night, coming home when the fireworks finished, then do it all again the next day, and the next—magic!'

'Drink your tea,' was Dottie's response to this, and Charles had to hide a smile. Had he just seen Jo get one over the indomitable old woman?

He sat between them, looking out to sea, unable to believe he was finally here—feeling again that slightly eerie sensation that he could be walking in his mother's footsteps, sitting where she had sat.

And suddenly he knew he had to ask. Pleased that he seemed to have been accepted into Dottie's household, he'd refrained from questions, but surely...

'Did my mother go to the carnival?'

There, the words were out!

'And why would you want to know?'

The words were icy, but at least she'd spoken. Now he had to find the right reply—he didn't want to blow this opportunity to find out something, no matter how small it might be.

He moved his chair so he was directly across from her, and spoke quietly, gently.

'I grew up knowing so much about my father's

family. I couldn't avoid it when their grim portraits stared down on me from every wall. But there was a hole where my mother should have been.'

He paused, but she was watching him.

Waiting?

'You asked me earlier if I had children and although I don't, one day I want to marry and when children come along I'd like to be able to tell them about their grandmother who came from so far away. How she met and fell in love with a handsome prince and ran away to marry him. But what can I tell them about her as a person? About her life when she grew up here, about what she liked to do, what made her happy, and what made her sad?'

He paused, waiting perhaps, but when Dottie didn't speak, he continued. 'You've kindly asked me to stay until I start work, so I'll be able to tell them about their great-grandmother and the beautiful house she lives in high above the Pacific Ocean. Can you see how exciting that would sound to young children living in a small, rather closed-in country in Europe?'

She looked away, but hadn't hmphed or said fiddle-faddle, so he drank his tea, aware Jo was as tense as he was. Then Dottie rose to her feet and moved away, turning back to say, 'Make sure you rub the silver cloth over the teapot before you put it away.'

Whether the order was for him or Jo he didn't know.

He couldn't think straight.

Then he felt Jo's hand on his arm.

'I don't know whether to laugh or cry,' she said shakily, and he covered her hand with his.

'Neither do I,' he managed, then they sat in silence, hand in hand, the tea growing cold in the cups, the silver teapot gleaming in the sun.

CHAPTER FOUR

'WAS I WRONG to ask?'

Jo and Charles were back in the kitchen, Jo washing the tea things, while Charles, having found the silver cloth in its plastic sleeve beside where the pot was kept, was polishing any suspect finger marks from the high gloss.

'Of course not,' Jo told him. 'It's the only way you're ever going to find out anything about your mother, although—'

She spun around, excitement gleaming in her blue eyes, while the echoing excitement in his body had more to do with those eyes than his search.

'I know she went away to boarding school, but that would only have been for her high school years, so there must be people in the town who knew her from primary school, and still saw her on holidays. Dottie will probably weaken to the extent she'll drop bits of information here and there, but I'm sure we can find out more.'

'We?' Charles asked, smiling at her enthusiasm.

'Of course, we,' Jo told him. 'You'd never know who to ask! How old was she when she left, do you know?'

'She must have been twenty-two or -three. She died just before her twenty-fifth birthday.'

'Far too young,' Jo said quietly, before she rallied. 'Well, come on. There's no time like the present.'

She was about to whirl out of the room but Charles caught her shoulder.

'Wait,' he said, and she turned to face him, so close he could see tiny freckles on her nose, see her chest rising and falling beneath the light T-shirt she was wearing. See the swell of her breasts, feel the warmth of her...

Whatever he'd been about to say disappeared, washed away by a great wave of...

Lust?

No, surely more than that!

Although it had been far too strong to be attraction.

'Charles?'

She was looking closely at him, and if her voice sounded a little breathy, well, that was probably nothing more than his imagination. Although the softness of her pale pink lips wasn't.

'I was going to say...'

He realised he still held her shoulder, and heat seared his hand.

'Dammit!' he muttered, stepping away from the source of his distraction, hoping that would help. 'I think I am losing my mind!'

'Going to the village?' Jo prompted kindly, and he glared at her.

Then remembered where his thoughts had been before she'd—

Cast a spell over him?

'I think it is a not good idea,' he finally managed, the words sounding stilted—foreign—even to him.

Definitely losing his mind!

'No?' Jo said, stepping back, as if she, too, wanted to avoid whatever minefield they'd blundered into.

He forced himself to think, to set aside whatever it was between him and this woman, and be his normal, practical self.

'I think if we ask around the village, it would get back to Dottie and I think that might be hurtful to her.'

There, it was out, and his relief was such that he smiled at Jo.

She wished he wouldn't! Wouldn't smile like that, wouldn't touch her to catch her attention. She knew they meant nothing, the smiles and the touches—well, her head knew that. It was just that her body was having trouble coming to terms with it.

Her body seemed to think that, released of the burden it had carried for nine months, it could go cavorting about however it liked.

Her body, she knew, was looking for more smiles and touches—*it* was positively revelling in them.

Surely pregnancy hadn't turned her into a wanton hussy?

Or was it simply that he was unattainable—this man who admitted he wanted to marry and have children.

A prince—but not hers.

No, her life was here in Anooka, her life dedicated to her patients, marriage and children no part of it...

But a flirtation?

Would that hurt?

'Well, what do you think?'

The question, coming what seemed like hours after whatever they'd been talking about, threw her completely.

What *had* they been talking about?

'If not hurt, maybe shamed in some way? I wouldn't like that.'

Hurt?

Shamed?

Jo's brain clicked into gear, and she looked at

Charles, who had crossed the kitchen and was wiping at a spot on the window above the sink.

'Of course she would be. I'm so sorry. I just didn't think.'

And now she had her brain back on track, she added, 'Anyway, once you start work you'll probably be spending more time in Anooka than out here. Do you have a starting date?'

He stopped cleaning the window and leant against the bench, so he was silhouetted against the light.

'Monday of next week. I gave myself some time to...'

Jo smiled as his broad shoulders shrugged.

'Get to know your grandmother?' she teased, then felt a little mean. 'Anyway, that means you'll get to see the surf carnival this weekend before you start work, and maybe on Thursday—oh, that's tomorrow, isn't it? The week's just vanished! Anyway, tomorrow, if you like, I'll take you into Anooka, show you around the hospital, and introduce you to the powers-that-be. I want to go in anyway, to tell them I'm available until my locum goes, if they're short-handed.'

'Do they get short-handed?' Charles asked, and Jo found herself relaxing. She'd rattled off the suggestion because she'd remained uneasy—unsettled—and talking seemed the best route back to normal.

And hospital conversations she could do.

'Here, the carnival starts the summer holiday period. In Australia, this dread custom of "Schoolies" has developed. Young people finishing their final year in high school descend on every beach in the nation—and many places overseas—to celebrate their new-found freedom. It's chaotic, though not as bad in sleepy little places like Port Anooka as it is in the main tourist towns.'

'They party?' Charles asked, and Jo smiled.

'Like you wouldn't believe,' she said. 'But thankfully it doesn't begin until after the carnival weekend and only lasts five days, after which many families arrive for their annual Christmas by the sea.'

'Christmas by the sea? Do you have any idea how exotic that sounds?'

'I'm afraid my main reaction to it is dread. The village trebles, or maybe quadruples, in population while, apart from casual staff in most of the shops, cafés and bars, everything else remains the same only busier.'

'Like ski season in our mountain villages—that I understand. One doctor who might normally serve three villages finds he's barely able to cope with his own, for these people don't leave their colds and flu and injuries at home.'

Jo grinned at him.

'It's all ahead of you,' she warned him. 'So,

tomorrow? Do you want a lift into town to meet and greet?'

Unfortunately, as she'd been doing very well, he smiled before he replied, and her body celebrated with more of those wanton flips and tingles.

'Most certainly,' he replied, 'and I would like to hire a car as well, so I can get about.'

Had she been so preoccupied with her reactions to Charles that she'd failed to hear Dottie come up behind her?

But at the sound of her voice, Jo started, and possibly let out a little yelp, although she hoped that had been her imagination.

'I have a perfectly good car you can use,' Dottie announced, sliding past Jo into the kitchen. 'Although, if you are working in Anooka, it's best you stay there. Jo, too, if they offer her a job. But you can take the car so you can visit me on days off.'

Jo was laughing.

'I imagine, Dottie, that's your way of telling us you're fed up with having us around. But you're right, it will be far more convenient for Charles to be closer to his work. And *so* kind to offer the car.'

Something in the words must have warned Charles what he was in for, because he frowned, then assured Dottie that it would be no trouble at all to hire a car.

'I may be based out of town for some of the time,' he said, trying to shore up his defences, but Jo knew he was lost. He was going to spend his six weeks with Port Anooka Hospital Authority driving a large, ancient, black vehicle with a rather unfortunate resemblance to a hearse.

'We're going into Anooka tomorrow, Dottie, if you'd like to come. Or if you need anything in town we could get it.'

'Anooka's too busy, too many people all bustling about the place,' Dottie replied, and although Jo raised her eyebrows, well aware how much Dottie enjoyed occasional jaunts into town, she said nothing.

'But if you've finished all your cleaning and polishing, which, I might add, pregnant women are supposed to do before they go into labour, not after, you could take me into the village now. There's no danger from the tides now, and I'd like to see if anyone has suffered or needs help.'

'That's a good idea, though I think we'd have heard if there'd been any major problems.'

'You make it sound as if this flooding is a regular event,' Charles said, as Dottie went upstairs to get ready for the outing.

'Maybe a couple of times a year,' Jo explained. 'But it must have been happening since the village was first settled because the houses and shops are built on the hills above flood level so it's only the roads in and out of the place and the sheds at the sporting fields that are really inundated.'

'So why is she keen to go?' Charles asked, and Jo grinned at him.

'She's a sticky beak! She might live out here in splendid isolation, but she likes to know everything that goes on in the village. She has a couple of cronies down there she'll genuinely want to check on, but her main hope will be that some of the buildings in the playing fields have been damaged.'

Charles stared at her in sheer disbelief.

'You're saying she wants to see them damaged?'

Jo shrugged, and smiled again, so all the symptoms of his awareness of this woman kicked in.

'Swept away more like. When her husband—when Bertie—was mayor, he arranged for the council to relocate some of the houses and businesses lower down the slopes—places that flooded regularly. Then he declared all the flood-prone land playing fields or parklands, so Dottie's been very peevish since various sporting organisations built clubhouses, *and* stands for spectators.'

'She hopes to see them washed away?" Charles

asked, his disbelief so great he momentarily forgot that it was Jo in front of him.

Until she smiled again.

'Bertie wouldn't have liked it, you see.'

Charles tried to take this in, even stepping back so he wasn't quite so close to Jo and wouldn't be distracted.

Something about this new information deeply disturbed him, and he had to work out why.

'Right,' he finally said. 'She was so besotted about Bertie she hates to see any of his good works changed in any way. But surely someone with that much love and passion *must* have had some for her daughter!'

He was watching Jo as he spoke, largely to make sure Dottie wasn't coming up behind her once again, but he couldn't miss the way Jo's lips thinned as she clamped them shut, or the way her eyes darkened with something he couldn't read, just before she turned away.

'I need to get my handbag from upstairs,' she said, then fled—or perhaps escaped would be a better word.

Something had happened and that something was connected to his mother. That was all fine and good, but if he couldn't find out from Jo what it was, he'd just have to find out some other way.

He'd been the one who'd squashed the idea of tracking down any of his mother's old school friends, but that might turn out to be the way to go.

Or could he persuade Jo to tell him more?

In time, when she knew him better?

Although he already knew her loyalty was to Dottie…

Dottie and Jo returned together, and Charles was amused to notice that for a visit to a village Dottie had donned a hat and gloves, while Jo had twisted her unruly hair into a knot at the back of her head, though from the wisps already escaping Charles wondered how long it would last.

But it changed her in some way, gave her an elegance he hadn't noticed before. It added to the beauty and intensified the uproar she so unwittingly caused in his body.

'We'll take my car, the Prince can drive,' Dottie decreed.

'But he doesn't know the village, and he'd be used to driving on the wrong side of the road. I don't mind driving, and we can take my car.'

'Don't argue, Jo. If he's going to be driving my car when he goes to work, he might as well get used to it.'

Jo shook her head, her disapproval evident, although there was a small smile playing around her lips—the kind of smile that made Charles wonder just what kind of vehicle his grandmother would deem suitable for the status she obviously felt she deserved.

Reluctance dragging at his feet, he followed Jo to the garage he'd already noticed at the back of the house.

It was worse—far worse—than he'd imagined: a great black tank of a thing, about thirty feet long.

'It looks like a hearse,' he muttered to Jo.

She smiled openly now.

'I think it was, but Dottie bought it because it was the only thing she could find that fitted Bertie's wheelchair in the back. The wheelchair folded up so she could take him to appointments—doctors, and therapy, and such.'

'It seems impossible,' he said. 'She's such a tiny woman, and the photos I've managed to see of him show him as a well-built man.'

Charles had opened the driver's door and was peering cautiously into the interior of the huge vehicle.

'It probably won't start,' he said, hoping that would be true so he could hire a small, convenient vehicle for his stay.

'You're not getting out of it that easily,' Jo said, grinning at him across the top. 'Dottie says there's no point in having a car that won't go so she has it serviced regularly.'

'She still drives?'

And this time Jo laughed.

'Not any more,' she said when she'd recovered, 'but that doesn't alter her opinion about keeping it serviceable.'

Charles shook his head—it was all too much for him!

But as Jo slipped into the passenger seat beside him for the short drive to the front door, he was glad of the size of the vehicle for it left a good space between them. Sitting in a modern compact car, she'd have been so much closer and he had already come to the conclusion that being close to her was not a good thing.

He was pretty sure the attraction had been brought on by proximity, and had decided that avoiding it—at least until he could work out how he felt—was the best option.

'So, are you going to start it, or just sit there staring out the window?'

As promised, the vehicle started immediately, the engine purring in neutral beneath the big bonnet.

'Just remember the length of it when you're backing or passing another car. The few times I've driven it—decreed by you-know-who—I was a total wreck.'

He backed smoothly out of the garage and drove sedately—it was the kind of car that had to be driven sedately—to the front door. Dottie was waiting for them, a colourful, Chinese parasol raised above her head.

Jo leapt out to hold the passenger's side door for her, but Dottie shook her head.

'If I'm going to be driven by a prince, I'll do it in style, thank you. I shall sit in the back and you may sit with me, Jo.'

Jo cast an agonised look at Charles, who just smiled and nodded at her, as if to say if Dottie wanted to play games, it was fine with him.

But how much would he take?

Jo had no idea, although she was reasonably sure he'd put up with a lot in order to find out more about his mother.

And Jo knew Dottie well enough to guess she'd be impressed by his willingness to go along with her teasing.

Which was all very well for him and Dottie, Jo thought to herself. But as she had already made arrangements to spend the next four weeks with Dottie, so her locum could have the run of her house, it meant—

Unless she was needed at the hospital. That would be the answer. Okay, Charles would also be working there, but they wouldn't necessarily see each other at all.

And there were four hospital flats so they wouldn't need to share…

Share?

Nonsense—get real here!

It was pathetic to think she couldn't work in the same place as Charles, or live close by, without going all silly over him. It was a medical fact that her hormones would still be in disarray after the pregnancy, and that explained the physical manifestations of attraction she felt when she was close to him.

Or, to be honest, when she heard his voice.

Worse, if he inadvertently touched her!

Get over it!

'Are you listening?' Dottie asked, bringing Jo back to the real world.

'Sorry, Dottie, you were saying?'

'I was saying—' her voice was icy! '—that the Prince drives better than you do. The last time you drove me to the village you jammed the brakes on instead of braking gently.'

Jo didn't have to see their chauffeur's shoulders shaking to know that he was delighted with this reprimand.

'You'll keep!' she muttered at him, then turned her full attention to their hostess, who was explaining the layout of the village to Charles, and giving him directions to turn left, or right, or sometimes both at the same time when she became confused.

The road had been cleaned, but mud from the flooded creek still lay thick on the sports field and the smell of it swept through the open windows of the non-air-conditioned car.

'If you want to check on your place or the clinic, Jo, Charles can drop me at Molly's and drive you around there.'

Jo had already checked that all was well at both places, but it was a good opportunity to show Charles something of the village.

'I'll be an hour,' Dottie decreed, once she was sure Molly was at home.

Being a perfect gentleman, Charles was out of the car as soon as it stopped, and opened the door for her, holding it open so Jo could slip out and into the front seat.

'She's certainly unique, isn't she?' Charles said, as they set off sedately up the road. 'Which way should we go when we reach the top?'

'Right will take us past the school then along the main shopping street, not that it is much to look at but it has the essentials in a general store, a baker, a butcher and hardware store.'

'And a café? Somewhere I could buy you a coffee, perhaps?

Jo was reluctant to admit to the café for all it was in a beautiful position that had views along the creek and out to sea.

And served fantastic coffee...

She was being silly, she knew. Sharing a coffee break didn't mean a thing, no matter how lovely the view.

'If you turn right again past the hardware shop, you can't miss the café.'

Now she smiled to herself, for the Seagull Café came as a shock to most visitors.

'Not the place with all the wet and miserable-looking seagulls on the roof?' Charles asked as they turned the corner.

'The very place! They're not real, although the ones that come and sit on the veranda railings and pinch your food are only too real. Kate, the proprietor, heard somewhere that if you put fake seagulls all around, the live birds would think it was the fake birds' territory and stay away.'

'It didn't work?' Charles asked as they pulled up.

'You'll see for yourself!' Jo told him, with a smile that brought goosebumps up on his skin.

Once he started work it would be all right, he was telling himself—when he realised Jo was racing down the path to the seagull-roofed café.

What had she heard?

Or seen?

He had no idea but he hurried after her, spurred on by the urgency he could read in her movement.

The reason lay just inside the back door of the café, a woman with a blood-soaked towel wrapped around her hand.

'The knife slipped,' she was whispering to Jo as he arrived on the scene.

'Dial triple zero,' Jo said to him. 'Ambulance and urgent.'

Charles dialled, pleased Jo had told him the emergency numbers, spoke, listened, thanked the person on the other end, then knelt beside the injured woman.

'Your scarf will be better than my belt,' he said, untangling the length of filmy material from around Jo's throat. 'There's so much blood it must be arterial and the person on the phone said the ambulance will have to come from Anooka so it might be a while.'

He was fastening the scarf around the woman's arm as he spoke quietly to Jo, who was, he realised, applying pressure to the wound.

But once he had the tourniquet in place and had noted the time, he went inside and found a freshly laundered towel and returned with it to their patient.

'Here, we'll use this—it will give us some idea of how much blood she's still losing.'

He spoke quietly but realised the woman was probably beyond hearing, if the pool of blood on the floor was any indication.

Jo lifted the blood-soaked rag she'd been holding, and he heard the hiss of her breath and felt his own chest tighten as they both saw the wound for the first time. No accidental slip of the knife, but a deliberate and deep slash between the tendons on the left forearm. The classic cut of a suicide who'd checked out a 'how to' page on the internet. And the tendons standing out either side of it would make it hard to stem the flow with a pressure pad. The tourniquet would have to stay.

Jo wrapped the clean cloth around the arm, which was seeping rather than spurting blood now, watching the woman all the time, a look of deep concern, even sadness, on her face.

'We could move her inside, make her more comfortable,' Charles suggested.

'Or make her comfortable here. She lives at the back of the shop. I'll find a blanket and pillow.'

Charles watched her go, and guessed by the slump of her shoulders her worry that, as a doctor, she should have known of the woman's fragile mental state.

Silly really, the woman might not even be Jo's patient, but she was certainly upset.

Be practical! he told himself, and looked around, taking in the mess of blood.

They could move the woman, maybe into one of the low-slung chairs he could see on the veranda, then they could clean up the blood.

Or Jo could watch the woman while he cleaned up the blood—put into practice some of the household skills he'd been perfecting at Dottie's place.

He lifted the woman carefully and carried her to the front of the café. Jo had returned and followed him, draping a blanket on the chair before Charles set her down, then covering her with a duvet, even though the day was warm.

'If you watch her I'll go and clean up some of the blood. She won't want to come back to that kind of mess.'

'You stay and watch, I'll clean up the blood,' Charles told her firmly. 'Just check her pulse from time to time to ensure the tourniquet isn't too tight.'

He went back to the kitchen, found cleaning things, and started work, and although he was meticulous, his mind worried at the question of why a woman with what was apparently a decent business would sit down in the doorway of her kitchen, quite early in the morning, and slit her wrists.

There was unhappiness everywhere, he knew that, but if Australia was anything like his own country, mental health services were stretched to the limit, and many people fell through the gaps.

He heard the ambulance siren and, with the kitchen floor wet but clean, he went out to wave to it so the attendants would know where to come.

They were kind and efficient, ready to whisk

their patient away within minutes. But as she was carried up to the road, she gave a cry of distress and called for Jo.

'The café!' she said. 'Who'll look after it?'

And for one frightening moment he wondered if Jo was about to volunteer his services, for she'd certainly looked his way.

'I'll lock it up now,' Jo told her, 'and then phone Rolf. He'll know what to do.'

'Of course he'll know what to do,' the woman said, bursting into tears. 'He always knows what to do.'

The crying became sobs that they no longer heard as the stretcher was loaded into the ambulance, which then drove quietly away.

'Rolf?' he asked Jo as she picked up the bedding and carried it back into the building.

'Ex-husband, and probably the cause of her cry for help, which was all it was, wasn't it?'

Charles nodded slowly. It was only one wrist, and at this time of the morning the woman would have been expecting customers, hence doing it at the kitchen door.

But that didn't lessen the anguish she must have been feeling to inflict that level of pain on herself.

He heard Jo on the phone, so walked around, closing and locking any open doors and windows, pausing to admire the view, regretting he hadn't sat there with Jo, enjoying a coffee.

'He'll sort out the café,' Jo told him. 'He has keys so we'll just pull the door shut so it locks, and leave it to him.'

He could hear how troubled she was, but didn't like to ask if she'd known the woman was unhappy. Maybe she'd tell him anyway.

Or maybe not, for they drove in silence back to where they'd left Dottie with her friend, and he followed her lead, saying nothing to Dottie on the drive home about the small drama they'd been part of.

'I'm going into Anooka to see how she is. I'll give her a lift home if she's okay to leave,' Jo told him when Dottie had gone upstairs to rest before lunch.

Charles knew he was frowning, but he had to ask.

'Do you really think they'll release her?'

That won him a wry smile.

'I'm almost sure of it. She'll assure whatever ED doctor she sees that she's perfectly all right, and that it was just a moment of madness, and because they really can't offer her much at the hospital, they'll send her home with a referral to see a psychologist.'

'But surely the hospital would have a psychologist or psychiatrist who would talk to her there.

The figures on people who make a second suicide attempt within days of their first are truly frightening.'

'I know,' Jo said sadly. 'And, yes, the hospital has at least two psychologists on staff but they mainly see outpatients, or give counselling to inpatients with serious conditions, and their families.'

'All of which is certainly needed,' Charles agreed, 'but still.'

'Let's go and see,' Jo said. 'If we both go then we don't need to go in tomorrow for you to meet the bosses and have a look around. I'll just let Dottie know.'

She was back within minutes, another bright scarf twisted around her neck.

'We'll take my car,' she said, leading the way back to the garage where a compact red vehicle had been all but unseen behind the hearse.

'We'll drive through the village and this time you'll get to see what sights there are,' she told him, 'then out along the river to Anooka itself. Originally, the port was to be the main town because in the early days goods came up from Sydney by boat, but after a couple of quite bad floods the town councillors realised that with such a narrow opening between the hills for the creek it would always flood in bad weather, and they shifted the town to Anooka.'

Was she talking like a tour guide to distract herself from sensations that being cooped up in the car with Charles was causing? She rather thought she was but what was the alternative?

No way could she follow the strong urges to rest her hand on his knee to feel his warmth, or touch the longer bit of hair that flopped onto his forehead! Was his hair a bit longer than he usually wore it, that he pushed it distractedly away, though he must know it would flop again?

She did!

Finally arriving at the hospital was a great relief, as she'd run out of tourist guide talk when he'd touched her shoulder to ask the name of the jacaranda that was in full bloom in a suburban yard.

She'd managed the word 'jacaranda', but the effort finished her and although she'd have been happy to have the prompt of a question, she didn't really want him touching her again because his touch warmed her skin and sent shivers down her spine.

Surely they'd need an extra hand at the hospital. Work would bring her down to earth.

She sighed as she finally found a vacant parking spot and switched off the engine.

Then looked at the man who was causing all the problems.

'If I told you I feel the same way, would it

help?' he said, with a smile so suggestive it should be illegal.

'I haven't the faintest idea what you're talking about,' she said crossly, and clambered out of the car.

CHAPTER FIVE

SHE LED THE way first to the ED but Kate was still in a treatment room, being stitched up, so Jo took him up to the admin offices on the top floor.

'I've always thought they should give the patients these views,' she said, as the silence between them was becoming uncomfortable.

But Charles was staring out the windows, taking in the town clustered below, then the green fields of the farmland that reached out to the rocky headlands and white sand beaches. He looked for Dottie's house, but guessed it must be further to the north.

'It *is* some view,' he said, but Jo was bent over a desk, talking to a young woman who was probably the receptionist.

'Sam Warren's in and can see us,' she called back to Charles, who was still taking in the spectacle beyond the windows. 'Sam's the general manager, and he handles a lot of the HR stuff as well, although Becky collates the staff rosters when they come up from the wards.'

Charles supposed it all made sense but as he'd had little to do with the administrative side of the hospitals where he'd worked, he really didn't know. He caught up with Jo, shook hands with Becky when he was introduced, and followed Jo into an inner sanctum.

'Jo, you're not pregnant! You've had the baby? Are you well? Please say you are because if you are, you're the answer to a fervent prayer!'

The man had leapt out from behind his desk and rushed towards Jo, arms extended, to give her a hug. And although Charles didn't know much about his own hospital's admin, he was fairly certain this wasn't normal behaviour. Although the man must be close to Jo to have known about the baby.

'What do you think, Charles?' Jo was saying, and he knew he'd missed some important bit of the conversation.

She smiled at him, which threatened to create more turmoil in his head.

'It looks like I'll be coming to work with you next week. I've still got the locum working my clinic, and Sam's desperate for staff in the emergency department. It's always the place that suffers most when something like the summer flu hits staff hard. The ED is desperately short-handed, especially with the carnival and Schoolies' Week coming up.'

Right!

The summer flu part of the conversation had given him a clue—the hospital was short-staffed—so he could understand this Sam being pleased that he, Charles, was starting on Monday, but Jo?

Sam, having shaken hands with Charles somewhere in the middle of Jo's explanation, had settled back behind his desk, and was now smiling at them in a kindly way.

'While you're in town, you might want to see the flat we have for you,' he said to Charles. 'Actually, Jo, it's a two-bedroom, if you want to share it any night you feel too tired to drive home.'

He peered at Jo for a moment, then added, 'That is, if you've got a home. Isn't your locum living at your place? Are you still at Dottie's?'

Jo nodded, glanced at Charles, then said, 'Charles is there too. He was blown in by the storm and Dottie relented enough to let him to stay until the water went down.'

Sam laughed.

'You mean she's dragooned you into staying, Charles. She loves a bit of company for all it tires her out after a while! She's probably about to kick you out.'

Charles blinked at this very accurate description of his grandmother, but Sam was still talking.

'She delivered me, you know. Delivered half the town, and still acts as if we all belong to her—scolding us if she thinks we've done something wrong, giving orders when she needs something done.'

That sounded more like the Dottie he was getting to know!

'Even if she's happy to let you stay, you should probably use the flat—Jo will tell you how unreliable our shift times are, and you're not so far away you can't visit she-who-must-be-obeyed when you've got time off!'

Sam was smiling broadly, and Charles knew the words were spoken with great affection.

Which was all very well, but sharing a flat with Jo?

He ignored a little niggle of what seemed like excitement and turned his mind firmly back to the conversation, which had moved on to practical matters.

He found, when he considered it, he would very much like to work with Jo, to see her in another setting.

But sharing a flat?

He tuned in to what Sam was saying—something about rosters…

'…try to get you both on at the same time. If

Dottie does decide she'd like you to visit, you might as well travel together. And it will save you hiring a car, Charles, at least for the moment, as Jo can give you a lift.'

Charles's mind flashed back to the hearse and he hurried to say that would be most convenient, super, in fact!

And if the twitch of Jo's lips and the twinkle in her eyes were anything to go on, she knew exactly why he was so excited at the prospect of travelling in her car.

Sam had stood up to come around the desk and shake his hand once again, fervent in his thanks, suggesting, if they had the time, Jo could show him around the ED while they were there.

'We're heading that way anyway,' Jo told him. 'We sent you a patient earlier and wanted to check up on her.'

'Well, see Becky on your way out for a key to the flat. It's the one with the green door. We're slowly doing them all up, thinking we might rent them out as most of the staff have homes in town.'

Jo thanked him, and they said goodbye.

But Sam was already dictating a note to his secretary—no doubt about new rosters and the extra doctor who had fallen, so fortuitously, into his lap.

While Charles's thoughts were on the flat…

Bad enough to be working with Jo, but sharing a flat?

The idea shocked and excited him in equal measure.

Was she mad? Jo asked herself, as the sudden jolt told them the elevator had reached the ground floor. Arranging to work with this man, who was already causing her no end of physical trouble?

And what on earth had he meant earlier—that bit about feeling the same way.

Of course it didn't help!

If anything, it threw her into even more confusion. How could he possibly know what she was feeling, let alone feel it himself?

How could a handsome, intelligent, worldly man like Charles—a man who probably called half the crowned heads of Europe by their first names—possibly feel attraction to a flabby, post-pregnant redhead?

The questions were hammering in her head as she left the building, a key with a green tag clutched in her hand. She headed across the car park, while the idea of sharing the green-doored flat with Charles made her walk even faster.

Until she was brought up short by a deep, beautifully modulated voice from behind her.

'Weren't we going to the ED to see your friend, and so you could show me around?'

'Oh, damn, of course we were. Come on.'

She spun around and walked quickly back towards the ED.

She felt Charles following her, her heightened awareness of him making her back feel uncomfortably…

Twitchy!

He caught up with her, which wasn't much better as now his arm brushed against hers.

'I think I should let you visit her, while I have a look around. She was obviously deeply upset about something and will talk more easily to a friend than a stranger.'

Jo glanced at him. He was right, of course, she should have thought of that herself. So why did it niggle at her?

Him being right, or the whole silly situation, which, in fact, she was probably imagining?

They walked into the huge room together, seeing patients scattered on chairs that were set in groups, rather than lined up along walls as they'd been when Jo was training.

'Looks comfortable,' Charles remarked, and Jo smiled. To hell with whatever was going on with her body, the man was an acquaintance, passing through her life. And in this case, their thoughts were on the same wavelength.

'I think the same thing every time I walk in here,' she said. 'I don't know where the idea came from but I'm sure the people waiting to be seen get less impatient because the wait is more comfortable than at a lot of places.'

She led him to the reception desk and introduced him, explaining he'd be starting here on Monday.

'Just have a look around,' the nurse on duty told him. 'We're so short-staffed I can't offer you a guided tour, but poke your head in wherever you want to and introduce yourself.'

'And I'd like to see Kate Atkins,' Jo said. 'She was brought in from Port about an hour ago.'

The nurse checked her computer.

'Doctor's hoping to admit her, but we've got one ward closed so it's hard to find a bed. She's in that kind of holding bay out the back. You know the way?"

Jo smiled at her.

'Should do,' she said. 'I've filled in here often enough and I'll be back on Monday too.'

She made her way out to the big room behind the ED, then peered through the curtains into the cubicles until she found a drowsy Kate, lying on her narrow stretcher, tears still damp on her cheeks.

'You okay?' Jo asked, and won a watery smile.

'For now, I suppose,' Kate told her.

'Well, that's the main thing,' Jo said. 'Go with "for now" and we'll sort out the rest later.'

She paused then gently touched Kate's cheek.

'We *will* sort it out, I promise you,' she said quietly, and Kate's smile improved.

'I know that,' she finally said. 'It was stupid. I felt lost—trapped—the busy season starting… Could I manage on my own? But now I know nothing's ever that bad. Thank you for finding me. I knew by the time you got there, I really, really didn't want to die.'

Jo grinned.

'You hold onto that thought,' she said. 'That's a huge first step towards getting to wherever you want to go. Now, is there anyone else I can phone? Rolf said he'd manage the café, but would you like your mother to come and stay for a while?'

Kate shook her head.

'Rolf will look after me when I go home. We've been best friends for ever. It was just the marriage part that didn't work out.'

'I understand,' Jo said. 'Now, what you need is sleep. You've got my mobile number if you need it, and I'll call in over the weekend, or come and get you if they decide to send you home.'

She bent and brushed a kiss against Kate's cheek, unprofessional for a doctor but definitely okay for a friend…

Back in the ED, Charles was waiting by the desk, chatting to the nurse.

'See you Monday,' he called to her, as he joined Jo near the door.

'It's a well set-up ED,' he said, as they walked out. 'I gather the hospital is fairly new.'

'Only opened eighteen months ago. The old one hadn't kept up with the population growth of the district, but this one's a beauty.'

She was reaching in her handbag for her car keys when she felt the other key, the one with the green tag, colour coded to the door.

They *should* have a look at the flat; check out what it contained in the way of home comforts if they were moving in next week. Yet the blithe way Sam had explained it was a two-bedroom so they could share had sent shivers down her spine.

She was having enough trouble with her reactions to Charles with Dottie around as chaperone. Heaven only knew where things might lead if they were sharing the flat, even occasionally…

'Aren't we going to see the flat?'

Trust him not to have forgotten it!

'Of course,' she said, clasping the key more tightly in her hand and striding out towards the back of the building. She'd done some time in this hospital before going into private practice and had lived in one of the flats, which had been behind the old building. As a very junior registrar her days had often been long, and night duty a regular occurrence.

They hadn't improved!

That was her first thought when she saw the rather ramshackle line of flats tucked away beneath some spreading poinciana trees, brilliant red and orange flowers just beginning to appear among the new leaves.

'Poincianas,' she said, before Charles could ask, but he seemed uninterested in the trees, focused instead on the end flat—the one with the green door.

Jo handed over the key, happy for him to lead the way inside, but of course, gentleman that he was, he opened the door and stood back so she had to go through first, passing very close to him, into a space that was neatly furnished with a three-piece suite, television, coffee table and a kitchenette at the far end. Two bedrooms, beds already made up, with fluffy towels folded on them, separated by a bathroom, led off a small hall, all in all a neat little place.

But not one Jo would want to spend time in—not if it meant sharing with Charles. The way her wanton hormones were behaving, she needed distance, not togetherness.

'Much better than some hospital accommodation I've lived in,' he was saying as he prowled around, opening cupboards in the kitchen and peering out the window that overlooked the paddocks behind the hospital.

'I assume we're to keep the key?' Jo said. 'Although, really, we'll need two—we won't both be coming off duty at the same time, even if we're rostered on the same shifts—no shifts ever end on time.'

Charles smiled at her.

'We'll be working in the same department. How hard will it be to get the key from whoever's got it—or even leave it in the tea room for whoever finishes first to take?'

It was the smile that did it!

No way could she spend her off-duty time in the close company of this man. She'd have to visit friends, or shop, or—

Something!

She was being silly. Yes, there was attraction there, so what harm would a little flirtation between them do? It couldn't go very far, and it might be fun!

Fun?

Was she out of her mind?

We'll need two keys,' she said firmly. 'I'll get another one cut.'

'That's fine,' he said. 'It's really no big deal and, who knows, this might be fun!'

'Fun!' Jo echoed, hardly able to believe he'd just voiced her thoughts. '*What* might just be fun?'

He grinned at her.

'Might take us both back to carefree, student days.'

Jo was about to say 'Hmph' but knew she'd sound just like Dottie, so she muttered at him instead.

'I can't remember too much that was carefree about my student days—more lectures and assignments and exams and always worrying whether I was going to faint dissecting a form-aldehyde-laden body.'

'So you never considered pathology?' Charles teased, and Jo had to smile, which confirmed her strong belief that sharing a flat with this man was *not* a good idea.

The days continued warm and sunny, and it was Charles, who'd been out for an early morning walk, who announced that the surf carnival people were arriving.

'At least,' he said, as he delivered two perfectly boiled eggs to Dottie, 'I suppose that's what all the cars and tents and caravans are doing on the far headland. Shall we all go?'

'Seen one, seen them all,' Dottie said. 'But Jo should take you, show you around. There'll be fireworks at night so you might as well stay all day.'

Disconcerted by what was really a dismissal, Jo was about to protest when Dottie added, 'Oh, don't fuss about me, Jo. You know perfectly well I can look after myself—even cook my own eggs when I don't have someone to do them for me—and Molly's going to look in later.'

'So?' Charles said.

And Jo, although every instinct was warning her against it, sighed and said, 'I suppose it's something you should see. We'll take our swimmers and towels so we can swim when it gets too hot, and hats, plenty of sunscreen, and the parking will be a nightmare so we'll walk.'

'Walk? But isn't it the other side of the village?'

'There's a foot bridge,' Dottie informed him, 'so people can get from one side to the other in a flood. Besides' she gave him a slightly hesitant look '…your mother always walked.'

Jo, who was quietly eating her breakfast, looked up in time to see the brief look of shock on Charles's face, and knew that this—Dottie's first unasked-for mention of his mother—must have struck deep. But he rallied, and smiled at Dottie.

'Then I shall certainly walk.'

He cleared his and Dottie's breakfast things off the table, and began to rinse the dishes.

'Leave those,' his grandmother ordered. 'I can still handle a little washing up. You get ready, and, as Jo said, don't forget the sunscreen.'

Jo stood up as he departed, cleared her breakfast things and, ignoring Dottie's protest, quickly washed and dried the dishes.

'I'm all ready to go,' she said. 'As soon as I woke up to the bright sunny day I knew we'd have to make the most of it. Are you sure you wouldn't like to come? We could take the car, and deck chairs to sit on, even a beach umbrella for shade.'

Dottie shook her head.

'No, you and the Prince go,' she said, 'and, for goodness' sake, have some fun. He looks as if he might be fun to be with and it's a long time since you've let your hair down.'

Jo had trouble processing this command, and she studied Dottie's face for a few moments, wondering just what the old woman was up to, but a rock would have given more away.

Dottie had been right in one thing. The Prince did look as if he might be fun to be with, and perhaps she could forget all the attraction stuff and just enjoy being with him.

Having fun!

They said goodbye to Dottie, who was in the living room, pulling dead flowers from a big arrangement and replacing them with others she must have collected earlier. Setting off along the clifftop, they dropped down as they came to where the creek ran out into the ocean and followed it along towards a small footbridge that was high above the now quiet water.

And walking along, with the sun warming her skin and the air redolent of the sea, Jo felt a surge of joy.

Joy?

The word that had come into her head surprised her but, considering it, she knew that it was the right one, for it was more than pleasure she was feeling. It was the bubbling happiness of joy!

'You look radiant!' Charles said, and she turned to him, stunned by *his* choice of word.

'I feel great!' she told him with a smile she knew was still in joyful mode. 'Just relaxed, and free, and utterly at peace with the world. I suppose the pregnancy might have taken more of a toll on my resilience than I'd realised, but right now I'd like to skip and dance and laugh and probably go a little mad. We're in a beautiful place, on a beautiful day, so why not go mad?'

They were under a shady tree at the approach to the bridge, and she felt Charles's hand on her shoulder—the hand that made the flesh beneath her skin feel warm.

'Just how mad?' he asked, a smile on his face but a distinct huskiness in his voice.

She stared at him, aware her words had been a little crazy, but as his head moved closer, and his lips met hers—just a brush at first, like a breath it was so light—then the madness took them and

Jo hoped the kiss would never end, that the madness would go on for ever...

'Madness!' she said, when they finally broke apart and she looked hastily around to make sure none of her patients were viewing this erratic behaviour.

'Madness?' he echoed, and she knew it wasn't. It was far more than that to her—something she had never felt before, not with anyone. Not that there'd been many 'anyones'...

But she couldn't tell him that, so she just smiled and said, 'What else could it be?'

What else indeed? She was seriously attracted to this man who'd just kissed her, but nothing could come of it—he was a prince, for heaven's sake—*and* he'd want children, which she believed, deep down and with utter conviction, that it would be unfair of her to have.

So, on her first holiday here, she'd settled on Port Anooka as the perfect place to spend her life. As the local GP she'd have a position in the town and plenty of acquaintances, and wouldn't need a label like wife or mother because she already had one—doctor!

They crossed the bridge while these thoughts tumbled in her head. Reminding her, reassuring her...

They climbed the far headland, while she considered whether having a light flirtation with someone passing through would fit into this life-plan and had almost decided it wouldn't when she tripped.

Charles caught her arm, held her until she was steady on her feet, and maybe just a little bit longer.

'You okay? You were walking blindly there.'

She looked at him and smiled, having done a complete backflip as he'd caught her arm and come down on the side of the flirtation being okay—providing she kept it light!

Maybe!

They walked on, dodging between the many small camps set up on its lush and still very damp grass. And when Charles took her hand to steady her as she stepped over another taut tent rope, she let it stay there, enjoying the connection to another human being—enjoying, if she was honest, the connection to him.

'Oh, my word!'

Charles's exclamation said it all. From the clifftop it looked as if the sea was alive with people. Lon boards, smaller modern surfboards and bodyboards, all were out, their riders taking advantage of the high curling breakers that swept in to the beach, while on the shore children played in the shallows, and the bright beach umbrellas looked like some newly sprung-up tent city.

'Quite something, huh?' Jo said to him, proud of the spectacle her little village had turned on.

'Quite something,' he repeated, although he was looking at her as he said it, and she felt heat rush through her body.

She should have brought the car—*and* the key to the green door! They could have this day—this one day out of time—and then forget about the whole attraction thing. It would be easier to forget after just one day, but after six weeks?

Impossible?

She didn't know...

Although even thinking about the flat with the green door was foolish, when one considered that she had given birth so recently. The baby might not have been hers, but her body still needed to get back to normal. Oxytocin might be helping her uterus contract, but it would take months of exercise to get her flabby stomach into shape.

She glanced at Charles, pleased to see he was caught up in the spectacle before them so wouldn't have seen the lascivious thoughts she'd been having reflected on her face.

They made their way down to the grassy dunes above the beach and found a space large enough for her to spread her big beach towel.

Locals close by called out hello, enquiring about the baby and how it was doing, and asking how she was.

Answering their questions was good, normal, and right now she needed as much normality as she could get. Some stopped to chat, and she introduced Charles, which was a bit of a dilemma as she wasn't certain Dottie would want him introduced as her grandson, so she went with the doctor who was starting at the Anooka Hospital on Monday and she was showing him the sights.

'They like you, your patients?' he said when they were on their own.

She laughed.

'I think all patients like their doctors, or at least pretend to. If they get stroppy with us we might retaliate by jabbing the needle in too far.'

But Charles was no longer listening. He was on his feet, looking down towards the beach, and, standing up, Jo could see a lifesaver on a jet-ski, trying to herd a group of swimmers back towards the shore.

'There is something wrong?' he asked.

'It's probably a rip, and it's taking the swimmers into the area where the surfers come in on their boards. With so many boards in the water, there could easily be an accident.'

'But, look, they have missed one.'

Most of the people on the dune were pointing now to where the head of a swimmer bobbed up and down, right in the path of a surfer on a longboard.

'There's a lifesaver in a tower on the beach, he will have seen that person and someone will be on their way to get him or her.'

Even as she spoke Jo saw the familiar red and yellow cap of a lifesaver in the water, no doubt heading towards the person in trouble.

'See the orange float he has over his shoulder? That will keep the swimmer afloat on the journey back to the beach. On the bigger beaches they are using drones to patrol the area, which also have the capability of carrying one of those floats and dropping it close to anyone in trouble. It's amazing what they can do.'

'That board-rider has gone into the curl of the wave, he won't see them,' Charles said, and before Jo realised it, he'd taken off, racing down the dune and across the beach and into the water.

Jo followed, more so she could yell at him for putting himself in danger than with any thought of giving help. The lifesavers who patrolled the beaches were well trained, and most clubs had at least one paramedic among their members.

Beside which an ambulance was parked beside the club—a necessity at any sporting event.

'They know their job,' she said, rather breathlessly, when she caught up with Charles. 'People drown trying to save someone else.'

She'd grabbed his arm and was holding onto him before she realised he was only in knee-deep water and probably hadn't intended going further in.

'I would not be so foolish,' he said. 'But that board was coming right at the swimmer and the lifesaver. See, that's the board coming in to shore now, but all three of them are somewhere under the waves.'

Four lifesavers were now at the scene and the jet-ski rider had gone out to stop the surfers until the accident was sorted. Now they could only wait.

The board-rider was the first to appear from the tumbling waves, followed by the lifesaver, helped by one of his mates, while another of the lifesavers now had the swimmer, holding him on the float as she headed for the beach.

The swimmer, a man, they discovered, was lifted from the water and laid on the sand, two of the lifesavers immediately beginning CPR while another arrived with the pack containing the resuscitation kit, the ambos following behind with a stretcher.

'They know their jobs and we will only get in the way,' Jo said to Charles, taking his arm as he made to step toward the drama.

He watched for a moment, then nodded.

'Like our ski patrols,' he said. 'This is what they train for. I—'

Whatever he was going to add was lost in an

urgent cry of 'Hey, Doc!' and Jo turned to see one of the lifesavers waving towards her.

She hurried towards him, Charles on her heels.

'Can you look at Susie's leg? I think the board caught her.'

A young woman was sitting on a towel, holding one end of it to her calf. Her swimsuit told them she was one of the lifesavers on duty, although she looked very young.

Jo knelt beside her, and lifted the towel. The fin on the back of the board had sliced her calf open, leaving a six-inch gash, deep enough to need absorbable sutures on the muscle before skin closure.

'She'll need to go to the hospital to have it cleaned and stitched,' she told the lad who'd called them over. 'Can you bring the first-aid box? We'll put a pressure pad and bandage on it then, rather than wait for the ambulance and the other patient, I'm sure you'll find a volunteer to take her to the hospital.'

'I'll take her,' the lad said, before running swiftly back to the clubhouse to get what was needed, while another club member sat down beside Susie to comfort her.

'Would you have repaired it at your surgery if you were working?' Charles asked as they stood and waited. And something in the way Jo looked at him made him add, 'I am wondering from the point of what GPs do—how far their duties might range.'

She grinned.

'So it wasn't a test of what I'm capable of?'

She was beautiful in his eyes all the time, but something in that impish grin stirred up all kinds of responses in his body.

Stick to the conversation, he warned himself, aware they'd already strayed into dangerous waters.

'Of course not, but would you?'

She shook her head.

'Something less deep—a clean cut even—but you need to think of the person. A surgeon at the hospital will do a much better job and leave barely a scar. For a young woman—for anyone— that might be important.'

He liked the way she thought, this woman, Charles decided, but surely this liking, this attraction was happening because this was his sentimental journey, and the romantic elopement of his mother with his father was ever-present in his mind.

And for all he imagined the attraction was mutual, immediately after having a baby was really not the best time to be considering any kind of romantic relationship, now, was it?

CHAPTER SIX

'I THINK THAT excitement was enough to put me off a swim this morning,' Charles said, as they returned to their belongings.

Jo nodded.

'Especially as the rip could get worse as the tide comes in. And given the crowds already packing the beach, a walk along it isn't too enticing.'

'So let's go back to the house and put up the Christmas decorations. I have noticed boxes of them in many of the rooms, and that Christmas tree looks sad with only one bauble on it!'

She had to smile.

'And what would you know about putting up Christmas decorations?' she asked, certain an array of servants would have done any decoration in a palace—not that she knew much of how he lived but surely there'd be a palace…

'Nothing,' he admitted with a grin so full of cheek it made her head spin. 'But if I am to learn of my Australian roots then I must learn this custom, too, no?'

'Of course, and that's a great idea. I was about to start when the water began coming through the roof,' Jo said, gathering up her belongings. 'And if we get finished in time, we can go to the coffee shop for lunch—Rolf serves the most fantastic avocado smash on toast and he'll still be in charge.'

She was folding her big beach towel to put into her backpack when Charles reached out and took it from her hands. His fingers brushed hers, startling her so she glanced up at his face and saw he, too, had felt that flash of something—almost like recognition.

He half smiled, shrugged, then bent to put the towel in his backpack—a gentlemanly act to lighten her load.

It wasn't the weight of her backpack worrying her as they set off but her physical reactions to what had been nothing more than an accidental touch. She had just given birth so, hormones or not, she was hardly in a position to plunge into an affair.

In fact, it was out of the question.

But a flirtation, that was different, surely. A few kisses now and then, touching, teasing, flirting. And if he made her feel more alive than she'd ever felt before, and sent fire racing through her body with a smile, then surely that was just, well, an added benefit—a reminder that she was, in fact, a woman…

She hitched her backpack onto her shoulder and led the way back through the crowds of spectators and campers, the carnival going on without much more than a slight delay.

But the light flirtation idea didn't seem so good as they headed back to the house. Walking beside him, aware of him in every cell of her body, was torture and she felt her tension building and building as they approached the tree where he had kissed her.

'I think perhaps we should kiss again, don't you?' he asked as they grew inevitably closer. 'Establish a little custom that is just for us?'

And although her nerves were screaming with frustration, her body demanding at least a kiss, she hesitated, suddenly aware that no flirtation with this man would ever be light.

But before she could process this, his hand slid around her waist and he drew her into the deep, hidden shadow beneath the tree, and, unable to resist, she let him. She let him turn her towards him, press her body against his, and claim her lips with a kiss that burned through any doubts and melted her bones so she slumped against him, replete for the moment, although she knew she'd want more.

Need more…

They resumed their walk in silence as crossed the bridge, and as they climbed back towards the house on the bluff Jo finally found enough breath to form words.

'We can watch the fireworks tonight from up here,' she said.

'Coward!'

The word made her turn to look at him and his teasing smile made her blush even before he spoke. 'You don't want to walk past the tree again! And what if I want to see the fun fair—I saw they have rides and bumper cars?'

'It will be getting dark and we'll drive,' Jo said firmly, and she stalked on ahead of him, although in two strides he was back by her side.

She'd thought hanging Christmas decorations would provide respite from the bombardment of sensations her body had been suffering, but no. The contents of the boxes had to be sorted, so hands inevitably brushed, and handing tinsel up to someone on a ladder meant fingers tangling—tingling!

They'd barely started in the living room when Dottie appeared.

'Do you have a special way you like things hung?' Jo asked her, and she shook her head, settled into a chair and watched the proceedings in silence.

Most un-Dottie-like!

With the windows swathed in tinsel and festive streamers, Jo declared they would start on the tree.

'That tree's no good,' Dottie declared suddenly enough to have them both turn and stare at her. 'It's too old, too worn and, anyway, Bertie always liked a live tree.'

'A live tree?' Jo echoed faintly. 'Does anyone in Anooka sell live trees? I can't remember seeing them anywhere.'

'Bertie always cut one down,' Dottie informed them. 'You know the kind, Jo, those dark green native pines. There are always some in that bushland at the back of the house. They grow in sandy soil all along the east coast.'

'I know the ones you mean. And you say there are some out the back? I must say I've never ventured far out there, but if there's a hatchet in the garage I'm sure Charles and I can find one.'

'Thank you,' Dottie said, and the words were such a surprise Jo could only stare at their host, who was looking out the window with a look of such sorrow on her face Jo wanted to hug her.

Charles had already picked up the old tree and was carrying it out of the room, so Jo followed, pausing only long enough to ask Dottie if she wanted anything before they left.

But the older woman remained silent, so lost in thought she probably hadn't heard Jo's voice.

'The poor dear,' Charles said. 'I suppose after Bertie had his stroke, she had to buy an artificial tree.'

Jo nodded, then shook her head.

'But she wasn't going to *not* have a tree! It's as my Gran said, she carried on as if nothing had ever changed despite Bertie being in a wheelchair.'

'*And* my mother being gone,' Charles reminded her as he dumped the old tree in a rubbish bin by the garage. He paused, his hand still holding the lid of the bin. 'I wonder if concentrating all her energies on Bertie helped her get over my mother's defection?'

'You're probably right,' Jo said with a sigh. 'It would explain why she looked so sad talking about the trees—your mother had probably decorated the ones that Bertie cut. She probably went with him to find the perfect one.'

'So why can't she tell me that?' Charles asked, and Jo, hearing the pain in his voice, took the bin lid gently from his hand, set it down in place and put her arms around him, offering a comforting hug.

'Was it very hard, growing up without your mother?' she murmured against his shoulder.

He eased her far enough away that he could look into her face.

'I can't honestly say it was. I had a nanny, of course, and I think most of the children I knew were the same. We were often brought out to be paraded before guests, or I'd be taken to dine with my father from time to time, and he would talk about the things I would have to do when I took his place. But it was Nanny Pat who brought me up, and when I went to school, so many of the other boys had grown up in a similar way that to us it was normal.'

Having delivered the hug she'd thought he needed, Jo had dropped her arms and moved a little away, but now it was her turn to feel sorrow, sorrow for a little boy—for all the children who had never really known their mothers.

Did her own child feel that way? Did she feel let down by the mother who had given her away? Did she carry a hidden sorrow for all she had loving parents?

At least Jo hoped to hell she had loving parents...

She thrust the thought away as she'd been doing now for nearly sixteen years and returned to the conversation with a question.

'So why the interest in your mother now?'

He smiled.

'For a start, I went to university where I learned that other people had real relationships with their parents. Would my mother have been equally interested in me both as her son and as a person in my own right? Would I have known her as my friends know their mothers? Or would she have been someone I ate with once a week, who checked my manners, and questioned whether I knew the order of precedence for seating at state dinners?'

Jo shook her head. She'd thought she'd had it tough, having only known her mother for fourteen years, but after a brief hiatus she'd had Gran.

But Charles!

'I'm sorry! We'll work this out, I'm sure we will. It's easy to see why you want to know more about your mother as a person, and you've come all this way and found a grandmother who refuses to mention her. But there has to be a reason, because Dottie, while gruff and forthright, is a kind person at heart.'

They'd moved into the garage as they were talking, and although Jo felt he needed at least one more hug, she turned her attention to the task at hand and found a small hatchet on the shelves, which the gardener kept meticulously tidy!

She handed it to Charles.

'Let's go find a tree,' she said. 'Maybe a real live Christmas tree will mellow Dottie into talking.'

Charles followed Jo out into the wild tangle of reeds and trees beyond the mown edge of the garden. They ducked under a branch of a particularly ugly tree with spiky, grey-green leaves, and large grey and bristly misshapen things that he imagined could give children nightmares.

'Banksias,' Jo said, right on cue. 'The flowers you might know as bottlebrush because they are exported as cut flowers to many parts of the world, but when they die they turn into one of these with those fluffy, beak-like seed pods.'

She snapped one off to show him.

'As children many of us were read stories about gum nut blossom fairies, and these featured as the big bad banksia men.'

Charles took the strange object, and could see how it had developed from a bottlebrush flower.

'It would have scared me,' he said.

But he'd lost Jo's attention. She was staring fixedly ahead, and as he finished speaking she murmured, 'Look!' in awed tones.

For there, right in front of them, was a small green tree, a perfect tree, about five feet in height, with its branches beautifully proportioned, and soft green foliage making it the ideal Christmas tree.

'It's beautiful,' Charles agreed. 'But should we take it? Is this public land? Or might it be a protected species?'

Jo turned to him, some of the excitement fading from her expressive face.

'Not public land,' she said, 'because I know Dottie's property extends right back towards Anooka itself. Apparently, Bertie wanted the land preserved as nature intended it so future generations could see the natural coastal scrub that grew in these parts before development took over.'

'It's certainly fascinating,' Charles said, moving a little away to a tree with strips of its bark hanging off it. 'See this?' he said, pulling at a strip of bark and admiring the soft pink colour of the inner layer. 'My mother didn't take much when she ran away, but she did have a small, framed scene of mountains and a creek and I'd swear it was made out of different colours of this bark.'

'Bark pictures!' Jo said. 'They were all the rage at one time. My gran used to collect bark when we were here on holiday and take it home to make a picture.'

Charles touched the tree, feeling the layers of paper-fine bark, wondering if this was the tree that had given its bark for his mother's scene.

'They're coastal tea trees but their common name is paper bark,' Jo was saying, but his mind had conjured up an image of his mother—not hard when his father had dozens of photographs—and now Charles pictured her by the tree, her hand where his was resting, and he knew with certainty that he'd done the right thing in coming here. He was learning about her, getting to know her, even without Dottie's help.

'Christmas tree!' Jo prompted, and he came back to earth to smile at her.

'It's perfect,' he said, 'and, better still, now I look around, there are plenty more of them, big and small, so they obviously regenerate well and we're not doing too much environmental damage to the...scrub? Is that what you called it?'

'Coastal scrub,' Jo confirmed, 'but you weren't thinking about that as you stood there.'

He smiled again.

'No, I was realising that even without Dottie's help I am learning so much about my mother. Looking at the young people at the beach this morning, from children upwards, they were all having fun, living such obviously free lives in the sunshine that I know she must have been like that. She would have swum there, played in the waves, maybe she rode a surfboard, then walked home along the path, sandy and tired, a little sunburnt maybe. She is coming to life for me now!'

With a lump almost too big to swallow in her throat, Jo reached out and took his hand, holding it tightly between hers, squeezing his fingers and hoping he'd hear the words she was too moved to say.

He used the hand she held to draw her closer, and took her in his arms, kissing her more gently this time, a long, exploratory kiss that started out as thanks that she was helping him along this journey of discovery and ended up, he hoped, saying much more.

For as he held her, kissed her, the vague suspicion that she was special to him—very special—firmed into knowledge and he found himself wanting her as he'd never wanted anyone before.

Was this what love felt like?

'We're here for the tree,' she whispered against his lips, and slowly he released her, looking into her face and seeing the shadows in her eyes, as if she too had felt a shift in their relationship.

'Cut it low,' she said, now totally in control while his head battled with the word 'relationship'. Really, it was hardly that!

He cut the tree and carried it back in triumph, going straight to the house while Jo replaced the hatchet.

Had Dottie watched them return that she was at the door to open it as he arrived?

'I've got a bucket of sand ready for it,' she said, leading him back into the decorated living room, then sitting again, watching.

To check if he was up to this?

To measure him against her beloved Bertie?

Jo returned in time to hold it steady while he packed sand around the trunk, but when it was done and she'd moved away towards Dottie to check it was upright, and he'd squatted on his haunches, pleased with his efforts, Dottie's voice broke the silence.

'You look like him, you know,' she said, and Charles turned slowly to look at her. 'Especially from side on, when he was young, when I first knew him.'

Her voice wavered on the final words and he saw Jo move to rest her hand on Dottie's shoulder, but the sight of the pair of them was blurry and he could find no words to speak.

Jo broke the still, taut silence.

'Perhaps you've some photos of Bertie when he was Charles's age that we could all look at sometime,' she said.

But Dottie had moved on—regained her composure and shut the door she'd so tantalisingly begun to open.

'It's lunchtime,' she said. 'Molly brought some avocados and we've Turkish bread in the freezer.' She turned to Charles. 'Do you like avocado?'

Unable to shift mental gears as swiftly as his grandmother, Charles nodded.

'Then Jo can make us avocado smash for lunch,' Dottie continued. 'In my day we called it avocado on toast but the smash thing seems to be all the go in cafés these days. And it is better on that Turkish bread, which we didn't have in my day. Just bread, brown or white, and now there are at least two dozen different breads in every supermarket.'

Was she talking to hide what she might have thought was a moment of weakness?

And was she a witch that she'd suggested the lunch Jo had spoken of them having at the café?

Charles sighed. How would he ever know? He was beginning to think if she lived to be a hundred he still wouldn't be able to work her out. But as Jo had left the room, no doubt to smash a few avocados, he should get rid of the bucket of leftover sand and tidy up around the tree.

They ate lunch under the poinciana tree. He'd been drafted in to move the chairs and table once again, but as he sat there, looking out to sea, biting into the crisp toast and creamy avocado, generously sprinkled with lemon, salt and pepper, a feeling of great well-being swept through him, and all the muddle of thoughts and questions in his head disappeared so he could simply sit and enjoy the company and the lunch, *and* the spectacular view out over the Pacific Ocean.

Pacific—peaceful! That was how he felt.

It was so pleasant—so peaceful—sitting there beneath the tree, that even though lunch had been finished for a while and the desultory conversation had stopped altogether, Jo was reluctant to leave.

In the end it was Dottie who moved first.

'You can't be hanging around here all afternoon,' she announced. 'You've that tree to decorate.'

She stood up and headed for the house, while Charles, housetrained in spite of having grown up with servants, stacked the dirty dishes on the tray and followed her.

Left alone, Jo would have liked to stay—to sit and think a bit more—but Charles was a guest and although she was quite happy for him to wash and dry the dishes and generally clean up the kitchen, she felt duty bound to do something about decorating the tree.

She walked into the house as Dottie zoomed up on the stair lift, surely at more than her usual breakneck speed.

Was she all right?

Jo hesitated in the entry, but as she wondered if she should go up and check, Dottie reappeared with a battered old cardboard box held in her arms.

This time she sat carefully on the lift's chair and came down decorously.

Once at the bottom, she stayed seated, calling Jo over to her.

'Use these decorations,' she said. 'There's an angel for the top.'

She passed the box to Jo and up she shot again.

Jo stood there for a moment, wondering what all this was about, then shrugged and took the box through to the living room, setting it down on a chair near the tree.

'Thanks for your help with the washing up,' Charles said to her as he walked into the room.

'Hey, I cooked,' Jo reminded him, and he laughed.

'Smashed the avocados at least!' he said. 'What have you got there?'

She told him about Dottie's behaviour.

'I hardly like to open the box,' she said, feeling again the apprehension she'd experienced as Dottie had handed her the box.

'Let me,' Charles offered, and he came to stand beside her.

'Be careful,' Jo warned, and he turned, grinning at her.

'You think it might be booby-trapped?'

'Don't be silly!' Her reactions to that damn grin of his made her speak more sharply than she'd intended. 'But the contents might be fragile.'

And fragile they were! Beautiful, delicate, crystal objects—balls, and bells, and birds, even butterflies.

Carefully they lifted them from their tissue paper wrappings, admiring each one before hanging it carefully on the tree. Light from the windows caught the baubles and made a million tiny rainbows around the pair of them as they worked.

'It's as if the tree knows where it wants each one,' Jo said quietly, as they neared the bottom of the box and the tree was evenly covered with the fragile objects.

'You're right,' Charles murmured. 'I've barely had to think before placing each one.'

And at the bottom, doubly wrapped, Jo found the angel, small and perfectly formed, with an inner ring of wire beneath the skirt so it could be fitted upright on the very top of the tree.

They stood back, shoulder to shoulder, ignoring the box of crumpled tissue on the chair.

'It's beautiful,' Jo said, shaking her head in wonder at the magic the crystal objects had wrought.

'Stunning,' Charles agreed.

'They were your mother's, yours now, I guess, if you want them.'

They turned to see Dottie right behind them, as if she'd just materialised there for they'd been too absorbed to hear the stair lift.

'I wouldn't use them on that artificial tree,' she continued. 'It didn't deserve such beauty—so I bought coloured ones from the shops and used them instead.'

Jo found herself swallowing hard yet again and turned to see how Charles was taking it.

But he had stepped behind her and crossed to Dottie, taking both her hands in his.

'Thank you,' he said, 'they are really beautiful. But I think they should remain here, and when I have children and come to visit, they can see them for themselves.'

Jo saw the brightness of tears in Dottie's eyes and waited, wondering how she would react.

'Well,' she said, 'they do need a small tree and you probably have an enormous one in your palace. But for myself, I've always wanted to see snow, especially at Christmas, with snowmen, and carol singers, and sleigh rides.'

'And so you shall!' Charles said, his face alight with happiness as he lifted Dottie off the floor and swung her round. 'You'll have it all and more besides. We can alternate our Christmases, one here so the children, when they come, know their Australian heritage, and one at home, so their great-grandmother can see snow.'

CHAPTER SEVEN

THEY'D WATCHED THE fireworks from the bluff, Dottie sitting between them in the deckchairs Charles had set up, eating fish and chips from cardboard boxes at Jo's insistence that it was a summer carnival must.

The fish, freshly caught by one of the trawlers moored on the harbour wall at the mouth of the creek, was delicious, the chips hot and crispy.

Charles leant back in his chair and watched the rockets shoot into the sky, bursting into brilliant bouquets of light that reflected on the water below so the whole world seemed to glow with colour.

He watched Jo's face, too, from time to time, surprising a child-like wonder in the gaze of this seemingly practical woman.

But he couldn't sit and stare at Jo. Dottie would be sure to notice and right now whatever it was they had between them was too new and fragile to be put under Dottie's blunt scrutiny.

He turned his thoughts back to his grand-mother.

Her talk of seeing snow at Christmas had come as such a surprise he could barely take it in, but she'd said it, and it could only mean she'd accepted him as her grandson.

It might only be a small crack in the wall of silence she'd built around his mother, but it was there.

And was he thinking of Dottie so he didn't have to think about too much about Jo—another woman he knew but really didn't know? He was reasonably sure the attraction he felt ran deep—but for a virtual stranger?

He'd picked up snippets about her life here and there, and seeing her around the house, watching the consideration with which she treated Dottie, he knew she was kind, thoughtful and very caring.

But why the surrogacy?

Because she was kind and caring?

And what kind of life had she led before it?

Hadn't Dottie mentioned a man?

A woman as beautiful as Jo would attract most men.

'...no work clothes here, and I don't want to disturb my locum and his family, so I might go into Anooka tomorrow and get some basic mix and match things there. The stores are all open seven days a week right through the holiday period.'

He'd missed the first part of the conversation. Had she asked if he wanted to go along?

The question lost relevance when Dottie said, 'And while you're away, Charles can take me down to the harbour, and we'll walk along the jetty, and I can show him where the big boats used to come in when the town was first settled.'

'Do you think she's mellowing?' he asked Jo when he'd put the deck chairs away and found her in the kitchen, making Dottie's night-time cocoa.

'Definitely,' Jo said.

'That was a "definitely" with a "but" hovering above it,' Charles told her.

'The "but" is your mother, isn't it? You're learning more about Bertie but, apart from the crystal ornaments, she's still tight-lipped about your mother, though it's hard to fathom why. Okay, so she ran off with someone Dottie didn't approve of—or maybe it was Bertie who disapproved. Maybe it was he who determined she cut herself off from their daughter, for all my gran said he was a lovely man.'

She sighed, which made Charles smile.

'There's no point in our speculating, is there? Let us just hope she continues to mellow, and drop tiny pearls of information that will one day give me a picture of my mother.'

'I think pearls make necklaces, not pictures,' Jo said to him. 'I'm taking this cocoa up to Dottie then going to bed myself. I'll see you in the morning.'

He watched her walk away, his mother forgotten as a new worry struck him. Had Jo been doing too much? Surrogate or not, she was a woman who'd just had a baby, and yet she'd barely stopped since the baby was born. First in her frenzy of housework, then showing him around the place, and now she was due to go back to work on Monday. Had *volunteered* to go back to work!

Was she keeping busy so she didn't have to think about the baby? Was she feeling loss, although she'd always known he wasn't hers?

Why hadn't he thought about it before, maybe talked to her about it—let her just talk...

He followed her up the stairs.

'You should be resting more,' he said, as she was about to disappear into Dottie's room.

'I'll rest tomorrow,' she said over her shoulder, and then she was gone.

Sunday dawned bright and clear and over breakfast Jo explained the hospital's shift system.

'Sam should have told you this but in most regional hospitals the day is divided into two shifts, eight to eight, though the day staff are lucky if they get away at eight, which is why staying at the flat makes sense. Becky emailed that we're on at eight tomorrow morning, and while I'm in town today I'm going to pick up some basic foodstuffs for the flat and a few spare clothes and toiletry items to leave there.

She spoke so matter-of-factly Charles had to wonder if she hadn't felt that shiver of excitement he'd felt at the flat—and did again now as she spoke about it.

He knew there wouldn't be a full-blown affair, not right now, but with such a strong attraction between them there'd certainly more kisses—mind-numbing kisses like the last one beneath the tree...

His brain was stuck on mind-numbing kisses so it wasn't until Jo had finished clearing the table and washing the dishes, and was about to leave the room, that she brought him back to the present with strict instructions to use plenty of sunscreen.

'Down by the harbour with the sun reflecting off the water, you can get very burnt.'

And she was gone.

Taking her neat compact car!

He was stuck with the hearse, although this time Dottie condescended to sit in the front so she could give a running commentary on the residents of the houses they passed—*drinks too*

much...lets her children run wild...has a lovely
wolfhound...that dog bites.

But he had to admit that the little harbour was
lovely. Fishing boats, brightly painted and hung
with nets, lay moored beside each other.

'We'll buy some fresh prawns and eat them at
the end of the jetty,' Dottie suggested, and they
did.

Charles was astonished at the nimble way this
new-found grandmother of his got down so she
could sit with her thin legs dangling over the
water. He settled beside her—the ever-present
'Did she do with this with my mother?' question
hovering in his head, but he wasn't going to spoil
the pleasure of either of them by mentioning it.

The prawns were fresh and sweet, the sun
spread warmth right through his body, and as he
wiped his hands on some wet wipes Dottie had
produced from one of her capacious pockets and
watched tiny fish swirling in the water below
them, feeding off the discarded prawn shells, he
knew he'd done the right thing in coming to this
place.

'We came here most weekends,' Dottie said,
'Bertie, Maggie and me. Bertie said a few hours
in the fresh air—even with the smell of fish—
would keep us all alive for ever!'

Maggie! His father had always called her Margaret, so this pet name was like a gift. He waited,

wanting to hear more but afraid to ask—afraid to push Dottie into talking.

'You'll have to help me up,' she finally announced. 'I can get down, but attempting to get up would probably land me in the water.'

'I'll lift you, that's the easiest way,' Charles suggested, and his grandmother turned and looked up at where he now stood beside her.

'Think you can?' she said, her smile a challenge, but there was nothing of her and he lifted her gently to her feet, steadied her with his hands on her shoulders, then offered her his arm.

He was inordinately pleased when she took it...

And the signs of truce were strengthened in the afternoon when he returned from a long walk south along the headland and back through the bushland Jo called scrub. Dottie met him in the entry.

'Jo's staying in town for dinner with some friends, so will I make cheese on toast for you for supper, or will you make it for me?'

Another challenge, but he gauged her mood was still amenable and suggested, 'Couldn't we make it together? You can grate the cheese and I'll do the toast.'

'Pah to grated cheese, sliced is just as good.'

But she followed him into the kitchen and pulled out what they'd need, handed him the bread and set to work, slicing cheese.

But his hope that she might talk more about his mother came to nought, for she worked in silence until they'd grilled the toast and made her cocoa—Charles making tea for himself.

It was then she said, 'I'm a little tired. I'll take mine up to bed. Help yourself to some books from the library. Bertie had some good ones on Australian history, and Maggie's head was always stuck in a book.'

She picked up her tray, ready to depart, but he took it from her.

'The least I can do is carry it up for you. The way you go flying up the stairs on that death machine, you'd probably spill the lot.'

There was no reply, but as he took the tray from her unresisting hands he saw the faraway look in her eyes and he knew she was back in the past, perhaps sitting in the library with his grandfather and his mother, both lost in books.

'Make the most of my last day as egg cooker,' Charles told Dottie next morning, setting her place at the table and pulling out her chair, while Jo fussed around, making lists of phone numbers and checking there was plenty of food in the cupboards and fridge.

'Stop that now, Jo. You know I've looked after myself perfectly well for years and will continue to do so until they carry me out of here in a box.'

'Which might be sooner than later if you don't slow down on the chair lift,' Jo warned her.

'Fiddle-faddle! Now, have your breakfast and leave me in peace. You're both welcome back when you've days off, but it will be nice to have my house to myself.'

Which mustn't have made Jo feel any easier about leaving her friend, Charles decided as they drove into town. Or was the tension he could feel radiating off Jo more to do with work?

Or the flat?

Sharing the flat?

As Jo parked in the staff area behind the hospital, he couldn't help glancing towards the row of flats, particularly the one with the green door.

'It's called plunging right in,' Jo said to him, as they walked into the emergency department. They'd come into the hospital through a side door, and Jo had shown him the lockers, the tearoom, and stock cupboard, where a supply of crisp, white coats was kept. He pulled one on over his T-shirt and jeans, adjusted his stethoscope around his neck, and followed her into mayhem.

The waiting room was packed, and nurses flashed from one curtained cubicle to the next.

'Accident out on the highway, mini-bus and two cars,' Fiona, who was at the triage desk, told them.

'The most severely injured have been airlifted

to major hospitals, but we've got six here, plus all the people who don't want to spoil their weekend with a hospital visit so come on a Monday morning.'

She was checking her computer as she spoke, and looked up to say, 'Jo, if you could take Cubicle Three, suspected appendicitis, and Charles—may we call you Charles?—take Cubicle Five, one of the RTA victims with serious cuts and abrasions, query damage to left arm and shoulder but X-rays should be back to the cubicle by now.'

Charles introduced himself to the patient, Ken, who was obviously in pain, his face grey and sweaty. He had an IV port open on the back of his right hand.

'Hook him up to a monitor, we need an ECG,' Charles told the nurse who'd been picking bits of gravel out of the patient's leg. 'Have you taken blood?'

The nurse shook his head.

'Then I'll finish what you're doing, you take a sample and get a rush test on troponin levels.'

'You think the shoulder pain could be his heart?'

Charles nodded, but as he attached the last lead and started the monitor for an ECG, the man stiffened and the monitor showed erratic rhythms then a flat line as the patient went into cardiac arrest.

Charles hit the emergency button, which had been the first thing he'd looked for as he'd entered the cubicle. He'd seen a resuscitation room on his tour with Jo, but there was no time to move the patient.

Jo came in with the crash-cart team and it was she who found the adrenalin they needed to get into the man as soon as possible to increase blood supply to the heart. Charles checked the syringe and used the open port on the man's hand to administer it, Jo already drawing up another dose for when it was needed.

The crash team had the paddles of the defibrillator set up, and the 'Clear' command had them all standing back, eyes on the monitor, waiting for the black lines to appear—hoping, praying for a regular rhythm.

Lines appeared then disappeared and the operator cranked up the machine and shocked the man again, and this time the lines came up and stayed there.

'More adrenalin, then we'll move him to the resus room,' a woman Charles now learned was Lauren, the ED registrar, said. 'If he's stable, we'll move him to the coronary ICU later this morning.'

She turned to Charles and introduced herself. 'You took blood?' she asked, and he nodded.

'Mainly to check his troponin levels when X-ray failed to show damage to his shoulder.'

Lauren nodded, then followed the patient as he was wheeled out of the room.

'Well, you don't waste any time getting noticed,' Jo said. 'All I've had is a suspected appendicitis who has gone to Theatre, and one of the RTA victims who's gone for X-rays—possible fractured pelvis.'

Charles caught up with Lauren as the patient was hooked up to the equipment in the resus room.

'I'll leave a nurse here but keep an eye on him myself, so check with Fiona who's next on the list. Hopefully it will be the child who's been wailing since he got here. The noise is beginning to sound like a drill in my head.'

Charles smiled, although he hadn't noticed the noise until she mentioned it, too caught up in the drama of his first Australian patient.

The child had earache, he discovered when he met Peter and his mum in a cubicle.

'Have you given him anything for it?' he asked the mother as they settled Peter on the examination couch so Charles could examine the ear.

'Paracetamol this morning at about four,' she said. 'He went back to sleep after that but woke up with it still sore so I brought him in.'

'So we'll have to have a look, won't we, Peter? How old are you?'

'Seven,' Peter told him, stopping his wailing so he could speak. 'You talk funny!'

'Peter!' from his mother, but Charles only smiled.

'I did all my studying in England and over there they do speak a bit differently. But they have the same instruments and this one's called an otoscope.'

'Like a telescope?' Peter asked, checking out the instrument the nurse had handed Charles. 'Only it's got like a little TV on the end.'

He pointed to the screen that would give Charles a magnified picture of the inner ear.

'That's where I look to see what's wrong,' Charles told him. 'Now, I have to move your ear a bit and it will hurt but not for long, then we'll give you something to help the pain and you can have the day off school. How's that?'

'Silly, there's no school, 'cos it's holidays.'

'Ah,' Charles said, pleased that the conversation had allowed him to pull Peter's ear gently up and back, and insert the otoscope.

'Maybe your mother will think of another treat because you're being so good.'

'Ice cream, Mum?' Peter asked and Charles smiled. Young Peter was obviously a child who didn't miss any opportunities that came his way.

'Your ear is infected,' he told the lad. 'We'll give you something now to stop the pain and some antibiotics to take. They will clear it up in a couple of days, but no swimming until it's better.'

'But it's the holidays,' Peter complained as his mother helped him sit up on the couch.

'Then you'll have to find some other fun, like riding your bicycle maybe.'

'Or my new skateboard—it's awesome,' Peter told him. 'It's red with a white stripe and the best wheels!'

'Sounds great,' Charles said, while behind him the nurse was asking Peter's mother about allergies.

'You really didn't have much of an induction into this place.' Charles looked around to see Jo standing just inside the cubicle. 'Lauren was going to do it when you arrived, but with the RTA and usual Monday-itis you were thrown in at the deep end. For antibiotics, we write out a script—there'll be a pad on the trolley—and the patient, or in this case...' she smiled at Peter '...the patient's mother takes it to the hospital pharmacy.'

She turned from Charles to Peter's mother.

'Do you know where that is?'

The woman nodded.

Charles wrote out the script and signed it, shook hands with Peter as he left, then turned to Jo.

'You were good with him,' she said. 'Do you like working with kids?'

'I suppose I do,' Charles told her, 'but what are you doing? Checking up on me or just skiving off?'

'I'm actually your supervisor,' she told him with a grin. 'Apparently, you foreign blokes can't just walk in here and start practising willy-nilly. You have to be supervised for a few weeks, or maybe it's a month, Lauren did explain. And because I'm just filling in as well, I've been appointed to keep an eye on you.'

'That *will* be nice!' Charles teased, and was surprised to see colour creep into Jo's cheeks.

Surprised, or pleased?

The question flitted through his head, but this was not the time for introspection...

'Right now I'd better report to triage again or you'll be giving me a bad report.'

Jo should have followed him, been given a patient for herself, but she felt unsettled. Had it had something to do with seeing Charles and the little boy that her arms began to ache and for a moment she felt the loss of the child that hadn't ever been hers to lose.

'Silly sentimentality!' she muttered to herself, as she made her own way to triage to find Charles had already been given a new patient.

'He's in Cubicle Seven, if you want to check,'

Fiona told her. 'Elderly woman with acute diarrhoea. I told him we should probably admit her.'

Jo laughed.

'I don't know what we doctors would do without the nurses in the ED. We'd certainly never manage.'

'Of course you wouldn't,' Fiona said. 'But right now, if you think the new bloke is okay with diarrhoea, you can see Mr Bell in One. His daughter brought him in, says he's got dementia.'

'Of course she does,' Jo replied, far too harshly. 'It's the holiday season and she'd like him put in hospital so she can have his house to herself.'

Fiona nodded, 'But we still have to see him,' she said, and Jo agreed.

She made her way to Cubicle One, knowing she could pull up the basic test for dementia on the screen in the cubicle but more worried about Allan Bell.

'Hello!' she said, as she walked in, hoping she sounded brighter than she felt. 'Did you not like the locum that you've come to see me here?'

She spoke to Allan, not his daughter, who was staring at her with disbelief.

'But you're on leave,' she said to Jo.

'And filling in here,' Jo said, as she took Allan's hand and gave it a squeeze.

'So what's the problem?' she asked him, but he

couldn't speak, the glassiness in his eyes revealing how emotionally upset he was.

'He's got Alzheimer's,' the daughter announced, and Allan shook his head.

'The locum at my practice could have done a test,' Jo told her. 'Why bring him here?'

Silence!

'I'll do a test,' Jo said. 'Would you like to wait outside? We won't be long.'

The daughter looked as if she was about to argue but eventually she flounced out.

Jo smiled at her old friend and patient.

'Well, now you're here I'll have to check you out.' She wound a blood-pressure cuff around his arm as she spoke. 'But you know this situation isn't going to get any better, don't you?'

Allan nodded, his face drawn with worry.

'You like Rosemary House and you've friends there, we've talked about it before.'

'But I'd have to sell the cottage,' he murmured, while the nurse wrote down his blood-pressure reading and swiped a thermometer across his forehead.

'It's *your* house,' Jo reminded him gently.

'But Barb lives there too now and where would she go?'

'She can find a nice flat somewhere at Port, or here in Anooka, or she could go back to Sydney and be closer to her grandchildren. She has plenty of options, Allan.'

'But she wants *my* house! If I sell it, she won't get it when I die.'

'No, but she'd get plenty of money when your place at Rosemary House is sold.'

Jo realised they'd had this conversation many times before but she persevered.

'Or if you're determined to keep the house, we can put in support services for you to make it easier to manage on your own, and Barb can go back to her family.'

'She won't!' Allan said dolefully.

'No!' Jo said, then dutifully pulled up the early dementia test on the screen, handed Allan a notepad and pen and ran through the test, altering it slightly as he knew it almost by heart.

'Is there someone else in the family who might come and stay with you, even just for a few weeks?' she asked.

Allan shook his head.

'Only one of Barb's kids and that's really what she wants, to have them all there over the holidays, but if one comes, they all come and that's five adults and seven kids and there's just not enough room. They have to sleep on the floor in the living room and in the garage. Barb says they don't mind, but it's too much for me to have them there for the whole six weeks of the holidays. I love them—well, most of them—but all of them at once, it's—'

'Hard,' Jo finished for him, although considering the size of Allan's cottage she thought impossible would be a more apt word, while the thought of an elderly man stepping his way over sleeping bodies to get to his own kitchen made her fearful for his safety.

'I'll talk to Barb now, if you don't mind waiting outside.'

Allan looked a little apprehensive, but stood up, such a neat man, well shaven, hair brushed back, wearing belted shorts with his shirt tucked in, leather sandals on his feet.

'So?' Barb said to Jo as she walked back in. 'I suppose you're going to tell me there's nothing wrong with him.'

'Not that I can find,' Jo said quietly. 'But I wonder if *you* need a break, Barb. We can organise support services for your father so you'd know he was being looked after, even put a carer in his house if you think he needs one there full time, and you could go down to Sydney and have Christmas with your family.'

'He's my family and we're his, and all the grandkids want to have Christmas at the beach. They want to come here.'

'Then they should rent a house—I know you probably won't get one now, but plan for next year. Allan's cottage is too small, and he finds it difficult when everyone is there, you must know that. So why not go to Sydney this year, then organise something up at Port for next Christmas?'

Barb's glare told her what she thought of that idea.

'So you're saying there's nothing wrong with him?' she demanded, and Jo nodded.

'Well, thanks for nothing!'

Jo watched her storm out, concern for Allan twisting her gut.

She could try to get a respite placement for Allan for few weeks, but when she'd done that once before, he'd returned home to his find his house like a deserted squat, and had been more distressed than angry.

In fact, having seen it, Jo had sent him back to respite for a week, while she and her fortnightly cleaning lady cleaned the place, even repainting a couple of walls the smaller children had drawn all over.

But right now she had to think about Barb.

She was muddling the situation around in her head as she entered the tearoom to find Charles standing by the urn, filling a mug with the steaming water.

'Would you like a cup? There are teabags and instant coffee but at least the milk is fresh.'

'Coffee, please, one sugar, no milk,' she said,

absentmindedly, although she did walk over to the cupboard and pull out the biscuit tin, hoping the night staff hadn't scoffed the lot.

There were four left, so she took them out, sharing them with Charles, who had set her coffee down on the table.

'If you're going out later for a spare toothbrush, you might buy a couple of packets of biscuits as well. There used to be a bottle for staff to put money into for snacks but they gave up on that and now whoever finds the tin empty usually buys new ones.'

'I'll do that,' he said, sitting down across the table from her. 'In fact, Lauren said to take a break now, because the worst of the morning rush has cleared. But I think there's more than biscuits on your mind.'

So as she drank her tea she told him about Allan, fit and spry in his late eighties and well able to take care of himself.

'His daughter used his age as an excuse to come and live with him—to look after him, she said, but she's never home, visiting friends or down at the club playing the pokies, so Allan not only looks after himself but her as well.'

'Is he managing that?' Charles asked, and Jo saw the empathy in his eyes.

'Just about,' she said. 'He's really very self-sufficient but come holiday time, she wants to bring all her family up to stay. Allan's cottage really isn't big enough and he hates having them all there at once, so she'd like him hospitalised—"for tests", she says. But it's mainly so her lot can have the run of the house, leaving their mess behind for Allan to clear up.'

Charles nodded.

'I imagine the mess isn't as bad as what he must feel when he sees how little respect the family has for the house he loves.'

'Exactly!' Jo said, and felt her frown deepening.

'So?' Charles prompted.

'I worry that she'll nag and nag and nag at him about it and it will wear him down—or wear him out so he does end up in hospital.'

'A subtle form of elder abuse,' Charles said quietly, and Jo nodded.

'Well, we'll just have to see that doesn't happen,' he continued. 'They don't know me, so I can turn up there from time to time, telling his daughter that because she had concerns about his mental health, I've been asked by the hospital to keep an eye on him. Tell her I have to make sure he's safe, and comfortable, and coping well.'

'Charles, that's brilliant,' Jo told him, smiling broadly as relief for Allan washed through her. 'I might even get my locum to do the same so she's never really sure when someone will come.'

'That's settled, then,' Charles said. 'So, moving on, do you have the key to the flat? I'll get some spare toiletries and things and drop them off before I come back to work.'

It's work, nothing more, and anyway the state you're in, what could happen? Jo thought as she handed over the key to the green door.

But inside she still felt a little thrill, so her hope that once they got to work the silly attraction thing would go away was well and truly dashed.

She'd spent the previous day keeping out of his way, telling herself it would be good for him and Dottie to spend some time together—just the two of them—but deep inside she'd been avoiding Charles, thinking a whole day out of his company might cool the heat he could generate so easily within her.

It hadn't worked.

Wouldn't ever work, she suspected, but at least she'd tried…

CHAPTER EIGHT

BY LATE AFTERNOON the place was so quiet Jo began to hope they'd get off duty on time. She thought of the basic provisions she'd left in the flat, then blanched at the thought of cooking after a twelve-hour shift.

Somewhere in the tearoom there'd be a pile of takeaway menus, there for staff who knew they wouldn't make it home in time to cook dinner.

'Are those takeaway menus you're perusing?'

She spun around to see Charles right behind her, and as her heart thumped and her nerves jangled she wondered how she'd get through the next two weeks, not only living in the same small flat but working in the same place as the man who was causing her so much confusion.

'For us to share in the flat?'

There was something so suggestive in his tone of voice she felt a blush creeping up her cheeks.

Ridiculous that a thirty-two-year-old woman should be blushing!

'Well, I certainly won't be cooking when we finally get off duty!' she said, more snappishly than necessary. 'Do you like Thai?'

She was saved from further embarrassment by a nurse poking her head around the door to announce that the first of the Schoolie patients was on the way in.

'He was crowd surfing on the beach at last night's concert but they dropped him and he landed on an ice-box someone had there. He was probably excited enough to feel no pain last night but it's got progressively worse during the day. The ambos suspect cracked ribs.'

'At the very least,' Jo said, thinking aloud while the nurse explained what an ice-box was to the man who didn't frequent Australian beaches in summer.

They greeted the patient together, speaking to the ambos as they transferred him onto an ED trolley.

'He's not entirely sober and not feeling well so I'd have a basin handy,' one of the ambos said quietly to Charles.

'I'll get one,' the nurse who'd called them said, and she disappeared from the cubicle.

'Let's check him over before we send him to X-Ray,' Jo said. She turned to the young man to ask his name and date of birth.

He gazed at her through bleary eyes but confirmed what the ambos had already filled in on the admittance form.

'And where's it hurting?' Jo asked, and the young man tried a rather twisted smile.

'All over right now, but I fell on my back, right onto the damn box. The lid was open and I got twisted up in it somehow.'

Jo was calmly removing his shirt as he spoke, and motioning to Charles to pull down his shorts so they could check his hips and pelvis.

Bruises were already beginning to spread up his body from the lumbar region to the upper ribs.

'F—!' the patient yelled as Jo touched his ribs. 'Sorry, but that hurt.'

'We'll ease your shirt off and a nurse will take you through to Radiology to have the area X-rayed. But if your rib hurt that much it's probably cracked or broken, so it will be very sore for some time to come.'

'But I'm only here five days!' he wailed, and Charles knew Jo was hiding a smile. Not because the young man was in pain but because of his priorities—having fun would come before any concern for his aches and pains.

'Will you see him when he comes back?' Jo asked, and it was Charles's turn to smile, but he didn't hide it.

'More checking up on me?' he asked, and to his surprise she looked embarrassed.

'It's just something we have to do with overseas trained doctors, apparently,' she said, looking so uncomfortable he touched her on the shoulder.

'Hey, I was only teasing.'

She turned towards him, said something he didn't hear—or didn't take in—because suddenly he was back on the walk home from the creek, thinking of the kiss they'd shared beneath the tree, thinking about how she'd felt in his arms, how his body had felt against hers.

He shook his head. Talk about inappropriate workplace behaviour! And he on probation!

He spoke to Fiona, hoping for another patient, but she told him to stay with Jo while they checked the X-rays.

Not a job for two doctors, but it *was* quiet!

Back in the cubicle he read what little there was on the young man's chart, finding out, at least, his name was Stewart, usually known as Stewie.

The trolley returned, Jo with it, and together they found the hairline crack in the eleventh rib, the first of the floating ribs.

'There's really not much we can do for you,' Charles explained. 'At one time the ribs were bound but patients then ran the risk of pneumonia as they weren't breathing as deeply as they should. The very best thing is ice—not on your skin but either using an ice-pack from the chemist or a packet of frozen peas, wrapped in a cloth and rested against the painful part for twenty minutes at a time. By tomorrow any swelling should have gone down, and you can use a heat pack—one of those you heat in the microwave for two minutes—thirty minutes on, thirty minutes off.'

'But I'll be missing all the fun,' Stewie complained. 'I can't sit around the apartment with hot and cold things on my back, we're all going rock climbing this afternoon and to the carnival tonight. Can't I just take drugs?'

'Paracetamol four-hourly,' Charles told him, and Stewie groaned.

'That won't help. What about something stronger, something with codeine or an opioid in it?'

Out of the corner of his eye Charles saw Jo give a minimal shake her head.

'We can give you an injection of painkiller that will get you home, after which I suggest you rest with the ice and then the heat as the doctor recommended,' Jo told their patient, with enough bite in her voice to prevent any further argument. 'You'll feel sore because your back is bruised, but that will settle down. The rib will hurt for weeks so be a bit careful about bumping into things.'

After he'd left, Jo explained.

'I'm not suspicious of that particular young man, but at this time of the year we get young people looking for opioid drugs they can sell in the pubs for up to twenty dollars a pill. The

Schoolie kids are pretty innocent, but we also get those we call "Toolies", who are older young men and some women who come back year after year. They hang around and take advantage of the largely innocent young school-leavers.'

'With drugs?' Charles asked, intrigued by this end-of-school ritual.

'Some!' Jo said.

'So how on earth can a place as small as Port Anooka handle this?'

Jo grinned at him.

'Did you see Stewie's plastic armband? As soon as they've unpacked, the Schoolies all report to a tent on the beach where their ID is checked and they are issued with a numbered and coloured armband. Over eighteens, who can legally go into a hotel or club, get a green band, while those under-derage have a red one. Because the bands are all numbered, the organisers have details of name, address, parents' contact details, etcetera to hand should anything go wrong. They know where each person is staying, and they give out information, particularly about a "buddy" system, where everyone has someone they are responsible for and who is responsible for them.'

'So you don't leave your drunk friend on the street corner to find her own way home to go off with a boy or girl you fancy without telling your buddy and making sure he has someone to see him home.'

Jo nodded.

'In the beginning it was chaotic, but now, thanks mainly to volunteers, it's a really safe environment.'

'Can we go and check it out?' Charles asked, and Jo smiled.

'If you can stand music that could burst your eardrums!' she said, while Charles battled his reactions to that smile.

'The council closes off a section of the beach and puts on live concerts every night, and only those in red or blue armbands can get in.'

'It's starting to sound like a good old-fashioned orgy but with rules,' Charles told her, hoping to win another smile.

But a buzzing in his pocket—he'd now been trusted with a pager—sent him back to the triage desk.

Schoolie number two, a young woman this time, red armband, vomiting and diarrhoea so severe her heart was racing from extreme dehydration.

Charles ordered fluids and carefully inserted a cannula into an almost flat vein on the back of her hand.

One of the ambos who'd been finishing the

hand-over moved his head to indicate Charles follow him out the door.

'We asked if she'd taken anything and she denied it, but I'd run full bloods on her just in case.'

Charles nodded and as his nurse assistant was still setting up the fluid bag, he poked his head out of the cubicle in search of Jo.

She was nowhere to be seen, so he asked the nurse, aware pathology departments had dozens of different tubes for blood collection, usually colour-coded for particular tests.

He was still hesitating when Jo materialised by his side once again.

'We have a pathology nurse, just ask the desk to page her,' Jo told him. 'They like to do it, and we let them. That way, we don't get the blame if things go wrong.'

He was about to leave when he realised he hadn't checked the fluid bag. He'd asked for something with electrolytes in it to replace some of those lost. The bag was the right one, so he titrated it to run slowly and steadily into the patient's body.

And now he could check her over more carefully, finding bruises on her arms and legs that were more easily explained by stumbling and falling than by being attacked. But why was she here on her own?

Wouldn't her buddy have travelled with her

in the ambulance, if only to see that she arrived safely at the hospital?

He'd no sooner thought about it than Jo returned, this time with another young woman in tow.

'I lost her,' the teenager said. 'I knew she was feeling sick and I should have stayed with her.'

'Well, you're here with her now,' Jo said. 'Do you know if she ate or drank anything out of the ordinary?'

'She wouldn't! We both agreed no drugs. Although when she started feeling sick and we were on our way to the first-aid tent, someone handed her a bottle of some red drink—said it would help with nausea. Could it have had something in it?'

'Possibly,' Jo told her, while Charles explained to the pathology nurse what tests he'd like to have done.

'And a general tox screen,' Jo added. 'Someone gave her something to drink—there's no knowing what was in it.'

'Would someone deliberately spike a drink with drugs?' Charles asked. 'The poor kid was already as sick as a dog—she wouldn't have been up to any fun and games.'

Jo shook her head.

'Some people don't care whether their victim is conscious or not.'

She sounded so upset he'd have liked to put

his arm around her and give her a hug. Actually, even if she hadn't sounded upset he'd have liked to give her a hug!

And *that* thought sent him striding away towards the tearoom—no, it could be busy. Maybe the bathroom, somewhere quiet where he could try to sort out what was going on in his head.

He'd dated nurses and doctors he'd worked with, but had never even imagined giving any of them a hug during working hours. Talk about inappropriate behaviour—and if it was bad here, how would things be at the flat?

It wasn't only Jo's physical beauty that attracted him, but some kind of inner serenity that seemed to him to shine from her. And here, seeing her at work, it was doubly obvious.

He stuck his head under the cold tap and rubbed his face vigorously, before scrubbing his head dry on paper towels.

Then, confident he'd managed to put a stop to his inappropriate thoughts before they got out of hand, he headed back to check on his patients.

'Snowing outside?' Jo asked, reaching up to pick a scrap of paper towel out of his hair and undoing all the good work the cold water had done.

'At home it would be,' he growled, and strode back to his patient.

She was sleeping, her buddy also asleep, sitting

on a chair with her head resting on arms she'd folded on the bed.

The nurse brought up the results of the blood test on the monitor screen and swivelled it towards Charles.

Jo wasn't sure whether she was being diligent in her supervision of the new doctor or simply liked being near him. She went with the former, because she didn't want to believe she was pathetic enough to be following him around like a teenager in the first throes of love.

Well, how she imagined such a teenager might behave. She'd kind of missed those years, what with her mother dying and the drama that had followed.

But surely she couldn't be making up for it now...

Whatever!

She found herself back in the cubicle with the sick young woman, and as the nurse had brought up the path results on the screen, it was only sensible that Jo move closer so she and Charles could read them together.

She'd done it hundreds of times with colleagues—read notes together—but all the other times she hadn't wanted to sidle closer so her arm could brush against his, and perhaps their hips would touch and she'd feel his body, his warmth...

'Nothing there?' she said.

Charles shook his head.

'Not even alcohol,' he pointed out. He left Jo staring at the screen and turned his attention back to his patient.

'Something she ate?' Jo said, being careful not to stand too close as she, too, studied the sleeping young women.

Charles shrugged and shook his head.

'It was a pretty extreme reaction. And if we don't know what caused it, it could happen again.'

He sounded worried enough for Jo to consider touching his arm—just as a colleague-to-colleague show of support—but the remaining shred of common sense in her brain told her to stop being stupid and to concentrate on the problem in front of them.

'What's your gut instinct about it?' she asked instead, and he turned and smiled at her.

'I was just about to ask you that but as you asked first, I'd like to let her sleep, and see how she is when she wakes up. I imagine as this is one of the first major events in her...' He paused. 'Would you call it her grown-up life?'

He was so earnest, so caring Jo had to smile.

'I suppose so,' she said. 'It's certainly considered a rite of passage.'

'Well, given that, she's not going to want to miss out on any more of it than she can help. So see how she is when she wakes up, ask her what she thinks, ask the buddy if she can manage, and take it from there.'

Jo nodded.

'And suggest she buys some electrolyte ice-blocks and drinks plenty of fluid.'

The words, though softly spoken, brought the buddy awake.

'They give out bottles of water all the time on the beach and on the streets and we keep drinking that, but I've just remembered she had one of those caffeine drinks last night. Could that have done it?'

Jo pictured the scene—the throng of young people on the beach dancing to the music, sculling a caffeinated drink to keep going.

'Maybe more than one?' she asked the buddy, who shrugged.

'We aren't joined at the hip,' she said, then began to cry.

'Most likely just exhaustion,' Charles said. 'I imagine they push themselves so they don't miss anything that's happening, particularly early in their stay. We'll keep an eye on her, let her sleep. We might even be able to find a bed for her buddy.'

He smiled at the still weeping young woman,

and Jo read empathy and compassion in the smile. It was true the ED wasn't busy, but he took the time to care for his patients as if they mattered as people, not just cases, and she believed that was the most important thing a doctor could offer.

But as she walked back to check on her own patients she wondered if she was seeing him this way because of the attraction.

That would be really daft!

She forced her mind back into work mode. If she just did her job, kept a purely supervisory eye on Charles, she could get through the day without making a fool of herself.

Probably!

In the end, they both got through the day, finishing with all Charles's patients being discharged and only one of hers—a burst appendix—admitted. But it was eight-thirty by the time they'd finished, and a quick phone call to check on Dottie told Jo the older woman had already had her supper and intended having an early night.

'You don't have to be checking on me every day,' she told Jo, 'and, anyway, Molly is coming to stay for a few days tomorrow. You and Charles just do your jobs, and I'll see you when you have time off.'

'She called you Charles,' Jo said to him, and he smiled at her.

'Do we take that as a sign she's warming to

me, or does she consider it more formal than "the Prince"?'

Jo shrugged.

'I was wondering that myself, but I guess only time will tell. But right now we need to eat—well, I definitely need to eat—so what do you like? Indian? Thai? Chinese?'

She smiled, before adding, 'I don't think Anooka rises to Livarochean cuisine, but it does have a Spanish tapas bar.'

'Let's go there,' Charles suggested. 'I'd be fascinated to see what Australians do with tapas.'

'Ha! You forget we're a multicultural nation,' Jo told him. 'It's not far, and a lovely evening for a walk.'

They walked through the balmy night to where a tall stone wall hid a courtyard lit by soft lanterns amid potted palms and bushy shrubs, already glinting with coloured Christmas lights. Tables were scattered here and there, and along a bar that ran the length of the building behind the terrace were wooden stools, many of them already occupied.

'We can eat at the bar or choose a selection of food and bring it over to a table.'

'Who would have known?' Charles said as he looked around. 'It's delightful. Let's eat in the courtyard.'

Big mistake, Jo realised a little later when they

were sharing a plate piled high with different tapas and sharing a small carafe of Spanish rosé.

The lanterns, the palms—it was far too intimate—the table small enough for their knees to brush together, and as they selected little delicacies on their forks and lifted them to their mouths, their spare hands seem to have taken hold of each other, fingers tangling in some kind of silent language.

His thumb brushed across her palm and the shiver that ran down her spine was so extreme she wondered he hadn't noticed her stiffen.

'This is very good,' Charles said. 'I must come back and speak to the chef. He must be Spanish to get the little delicacies just right.'

'If Alejandro is a Spanish name then he certainly is, although he has been here for a long time.'

They finished the meal, with Charles insisting he pay the bill, then wandered back to the hospital hand in hand, although Jo wasn't sure how that had happened.

And as they drew closer to the flat, in the shadow of the poinciana tree, he put his arm around her shoulder, and when she didn't object, he drew her closer, wanting to feel her body pressed to his, to feed off her warmth, to pick up the scent of her, arousing excitement through his body.

And through hers?

He had no idea, although he suspected this attraction wasn't all one-sided, especially not if her reaction to his kisses were any guide.

But just to make sure, as they reached the door of the flat he turned her in his arms and brushed his lips across hers. Her response was immediate, a kiss that numbed his lips and set his groin on fire. Her arms were tight around his shoulders, fingers pushing into his hair, her body pressed to his as if seeking to fill every crevice with his warmth.

At length, she slumped against him, arms still around his neck as if she needed to hold onto him for support.

'You have no idea how much I needed that,' she muttered against his neck. 'All day at work, sitting in the restaurant, walking back, and every moment wanting to kiss you, to feel your body against mine, to touch your arm, your cheek—I can't believe it's all so desperate. It *has* to be the pregnancy—the hormones it released.'

He tipped her head back and smiled into her flushed face.

'Because the alternative is that you're a sex-crazed woman who'd leap on any available man?'

He felt the sigh that filled her chest before slithering from her lips.

'I'm not sure that they'd even have to be available,' she said, looking so downhearted he had to kiss her again.

'Best we go in before someone comes into the car park and sees two doctors carrying on in public,' she said when they broke apart again.

But when they entered the flat he knew that something had changed—that Jo had drawn back from him.

Regretting her admission that she'd needed the kiss so badly?

Now she was talking about Dottie, about the house, and the roof and how she'd have to ask around at the hospital to see if they could get someone who would fix it.

The words—the suggestions—all made sense, but he knew beneath them she was lost in some dark or maybe far-off place. He felt a sense of frustration that he didn't know her better, hadn't known her longer, couldn't even guess at her thoughts and feelings.

Except when she was kissing him!

CHAPTER NINE

SHE SHOULDN'T KEEP on kissing him, Jo thought as Charles wandered around the flat, touching surfaces, opening cupboards.

She knew she'd cut him off when they'd come in, but the kiss, and her confession that she'd wanted it all day, had made her feel very uncomfortable.

It wasn't that she was initiating the kisses, which would be a very forward thing to do, as her gran would have said, but she'd definitely been responding, although responding barely covered the passion with which she'd met his kiss.

And kissed him back…

The kisses had left her hot and flustered, and slightly wobbly at the knees, yet Charles seemed unaffected. Hadn't he simply taken the key from her unresisting hand and opened the flat door?

As if he'd guessed at the emotional storm inside her.

Heaven help her if that was the case—if he

was perceptive enough to realise the effect he had on her…

She'd be like putty in his hands, and if he stayed six more weeks, and her body had returned to more or less normal, there'd be no way she wouldn't end up in his bed.

Maybe he wouldn't stay and, anyway, would he really want her in that way? It was one thing to exchange a couple of almost chaste kisses—well, not very chaste…actually quite hot—but he had a position to uphold and was probably very wary about whom he took to bed, and when, and she doubted a flabby, post-delivery woman would be his first choice.

So maybe she'd just consider it kissing practice, like getting back on a horse after a fall—yes, that was how she'd look at it.

In the meantime, they had to settle into their temporary quarters—and how awkward was that likely to be?

Perhaps it would be best to get it out into the open.

Well, anything would be better than the tension she was feeling, alone in the flat with Charles.

'I'm sure it's only proximity,' she said, aware her voice sounded as strained as she felt. 'We've been thrown together, first by the weather and now with work and the flat. Proximity, that's all this is.'

Even to herself it didn't make sense so when Charles crossed the room towards her, cupped her cheek in his hand and said, 'What "this"?' she had no idea how to answer him.

She stood, rooted to the spot, the warmth of his hand on her cheek sending sparks of agitation through her body. And short of throwing herself into his arms to show him what 'this' she meant, she had no idea.

But the wretched the man was waiting for an answer, and making matters worse by smiling at her.

Or at her confusion!

'The attraction thing!'

She all but spat the words at him, annoyed at being put on the spot, although she'd brought his question on herself.

She stepped away, forcing him back, and crossed to the kitchen window that looked out over the scrub. She felt him come up behind her, not touching, just being there...

'I think you know as well as I do that it's not proximity, this attraction between us, but something real and strong and, to me, quite shocking in its intensity, given how quickly it sprang into being.'

He touched her shoulder, turned her, kissed her gently on the lips—a quiet kiss, no pressure, but saying so much more than words ever could.

Or was she imagining it?

'I'm lost!' she admitted, needing to get this almost-relationship out into the open. 'I've no idea where this can go. If I hadn't just had a baby, making it unfeasible for us to go to bed together, we could have had a short affair, you'd go back to Livaroche, and I'd get on with my life. Do you think it's *because* we can't go to bed together right now that the attraction seems so strong?'

Charles drew her close, his arms around her back, holding her to him, as he said quietly, 'Could it not be more complicated than attraction?'

'More complicated than attraction?' Jo echoed. 'I would have thought attraction was complicated enough.'

'And love?'

Jo stepped back, breaking the loose hold he'd had on her body.

'Love?' Another echo! 'How could it possibly be love? You're a prince, you need a princess, or someone close to princess status at least. You can't go falling in love with a redheaded nobody from a village so small it's not on most maps. Besides which you barely know me, *and* I threw a bucket of water over you.'

He'd taken her hands so she couldn't back away further.

'I think it was the bucket of water that did it for me,' he said, laughter gleaming in his eyes.

Jo shook her head.

Love?

He *had* to be joking!

'I have to go to bed. It's after midnight and we've work tomorrow. I put my things in the front room, so you can have the back. I'll just have a quick shower and get out of your way.'

She could hear the words tumbling over each other as they left her lips, and hoped they were making sense.

Charles watched her go then turned back to look out the window, over the dark shadows of trees and bushes that made up the scrub, and tried to think.

To make sense of his emotions…

To separate them from his reason for being here, his search for knowledge of his mother.

Was his attraction to Jo something to do with that? A romantic hangover from his father's tales of love…?

Was he subconsciously trying to replicate those stories?

He didn't know, although deep down he doubted the answer was so simple.

Deep down, there was a sureness that Jo was something special—something special to him and for him.

Love?

He shook his head, heard her soft, 'Goodnight,' as she flitted from bathroom to bedroom, determined not to turn and look, to catch one last glimpse before she went to bed.

And he certainly wasn't going to think about beds in conjunction with Jo Wainwright—that way lay madness...

But she would soon be gone. The baby was supposed to have been born on Christmas Day and probably she'd booked the locum for a week or two after that, which left four days to Christmas, and another, maybe ten, then she'd no longer be working at the hospital, or living at Dottie's, and he needn't see her again.

But far from cheering him up, that idea left him feeling slightly ill, so he pushed it all out of his head and headed for his bedroom to collect a pair of boxers as he was pretty sure his habit of sleeping in the nude would *not* be a good idea in this small flat.

Work was the answer!

He'd throw himself into work, and when he had no patients to see, he'd explore the hospital, talk to the nurses and doctors, learn how the system worked.

They'd still be sharing the flat, but he could handle that.

Or so he thought until he entered the bathroom

and a scent that was probably no more than soap, yet was quintessentially Jo, lingered there, and his body responded immediately.

At least he was in the right place for a cold shower…

Had their thinking been along the same lines that the first thing she said to him next morning was, 'I've phoned the hospital to tell them I'll be late— I have to go out to Port and sign some papers at the surgery.'

He'd been up for some time, taken a walk along a track behind the flats and been surprised to find the ocean at the end of it. Somehow he'd imagined they were further inland.

Now he was at the kitchen table, spreading marmalade on his toast, when she'd poked her head out the door and spoken to him.

'No worries,' he said, using the expression he had heard so often at the hospital the previous day.

Empty the bedpan—no worries. Do an extra shift—no worries. Crash cart? No worries!

They definitely weren't lackadaisical people, for they performed all their duties with swift efficiency, but it seemed to him, on such short acquaintance, that no one ever got flustered.

Laid-back! That was the word.

Well, he was pretty sure he could do laid-back as well as the next person.

Until Jo came out of the bedroom wearing a lemon dress that emphasised her still considerably lush breasts, trim waist and long slim legs.

Definitely not laid-back—more gobsmacked.

Because he'd never seen her in a dress?

And here she was, all woman in sunshiny yellow, stirring every nerve in his body into a kind of longing he'd never felt before.

He couldn't have felt it before or he'd have remembered.

Had he gone pale that the vision in yellow said, 'I won't be too late,' in a kind, reassuring, doctor-to-patient voice, and before he found his own voice she'd disappeared.

Well, that was one night in the flat he'd survived, he thought gloomily as he made his way over to the hospital, aware he should be glad Jo wouldn't be there for a while, and yet already—

Missing her?

Ridiculous!

Fiona's smile was enough to bring him back to earth and cheer him up, because she was obviously delighted to see him.

'Would you mind seeing Mr Bell? He's Fiona's patient really, but she's not in until later, and he's really not very well. Cubicle Two.'

Mr Bell?

Was this the elderly man Jo had been concerned about?'

He'd no more than set one foot inside the cubicle than the woman sitting by the patient began to talk.

'I told Jo he was no good—but, oh, no, she knew best. She sent him home and now look at him.'

Mr Ball did indeed look bad. He had a huge bruise on one side of his face, older than his other contusions for it was already turning yellow. And the smell emanating from him suggested he'd urinated on himself.

Charles introduced himself and explained that Jo wasn't in.

'Thank heaven!' muttered the woman Charles took to be the daughter.

'Would you mind waiting outside while I examine your—father, is it?'

'Yes, and I'm his only daughter and closest relative, not to mention having to be his full-time carer.'

'Yes, well, if you could wait outside I'll come and get you when I've finished.

The nurse was carefully peeling back Mr Bell's shirt, revealing yet more bruises.

'Barb says I fell,' the old man said. 'But I've never fallen before, not in all the time I've lived by myself.'

Jo had suspected elder abuse, but what to do? It had obviously got out of hand this time. Very gently he palpated the old man's ribs, feeling for any movement as a broken rib could damage the lungs and cause a multitude of problems. Everything seemed intact but an X-ray would confirm it.

Moving down the body, he found a vivid red abrasion across the lower abdomen. Could the old man have been tied up? Tied to a chair perhaps?

Feeling quite ill as he continued to examine the injuries, he was relieved when Jo walked in.

'Oh, Allan, what has happened to you?' Jo asked, taking one of the old man's hands in hers.

'I'm sure Barb didn't mean it,' he said. 'I must have fallen and hit my cheek' he pressed a gnarled hand to where a clear handprint was visible '… and she decided I'd be safer if she tied me in my chair, not tight, mind you, but she went out and I had to—well, you know my bladder isn't very strong—and when she came home she was so angry, and said I couldn't live at home any more and brought me here.'

Jo shook her head and looked at Charles, who had no idea what to suggest, except they couldn't send him home with that harridan.

'We'll sort it,' Jo said gently to the older man, and Charles knew from the determined glint in her eyes that it didn't bode well for Barb! 'We'll get you X-rayed to make sure there's nothing broken, then how about I find a carer to move in with you? Just till after Christmas. Those ten days people get off around Christmastime is when Barb wants all her family there, and if a carer is around to keep an eye on you, she can go down south to them for a change.'

'Oh, Jo, could you really fix that for me?' Mr Bell asked.

'Of course I can, I'll get straight onto it. Now, I'll hand you back to Dr Charles to organise some X-rays and I'll talk to Barb—tell her you need medical attention for a few weeks and a carer can give it to you. I'll tell her that if a trained carer is living there, her reports will make it easier for me to tell if you're losing your marbles—that should go down a treat!'

Jo was smiling but Charles could see the anger in her eyes, sheer fury that anyone could treat an old man like this.

He organised an orderly to take Mr Bell to X-Ray, then went back to Fiona for a new patient, pausing only briefly on the way to eavesdrop on Jo's conversation with the implacable Barb.

But Jo was standing no nonsense.

'You know there are only two bedrooms in the cottage and I'll need the other one for the carer. Why not take the opportunity to have Christmas with your family?'

'I could have Christmas with my family right

here if that old man wasn't so stubborn.' Barb spat the words at Jo, but she remained calm, although Charles guessed she was reining in her temper with difficulty.

'Did you win?' he asked Jo later.

'*And* got her a seat on this afternoon's flight,' Jo said, but there was little triumph in her tone.

'It just shouldn't happen, Charles,' she said. 'Allan's been nothing but kind and generous to Barb and she treats him like that.'

'Should we keep him in hospital overnight?' She nodded.

'I think so. Just in case there's some kidney damage or something else we don't know about. And it will give me a chance to get someone in to clean his cottage and find a carer who'll feed him decently. He's practically skin and bone.'

Jo left Charles to check Allan's X-rays, clean up his wounds, and admit him overnight for observation, and reported to the triage desk

But the usual steady stream of patients failed to materialise, and the regular staff decided to pull out their Christmas decorations, so Jo was struggling to attach a lot of disparate branches to a plastic Christmas tree in such a way it looked approximately the right shape when Charles appeared, having personally delivered Allan Bell to a ward for observation.

'Are you sure that's how it's supposed to look?' he asked Jo as he walked around the battered tree to get the full three-sixty-degree experience.

'No, of course I'm not,' she snapped at him, thrusting a bunch of branches into his hands. 'You have a go!'

'Huffy, huh?' a passing nurse said, and Jo sent her a glare that would have melted ice.

'I volunteered to help out with patients,' she muttered. 'I shouldn't have to be doing this!'

'Then leave it to me,' Charles told her. 'You might be better at hanging tinsel, although the person currently doing that is about to be decapitated by the ceiling fan.'

By the end of the day, between patients, the staff had filled the ED with Christmas spirit, from the tree Charles had managed to assemble perfectly to fake pine branches along the window sills.

Jo met Charles in the staffroom.

'I've just been visiting Allan,' she said. 'I was feeling bad because I'd threatened getting the police if Barb didn't get on the Sydney flight, but when he told me a little more of what had happened, I was almost sorry I hadn't put in a complaint.'

'Did she hit him?' Charles asked, and Jo shook her head.

'Allan's too loyal to say so, but that's a palm

print across his face—a palm complete with fingers—and it must have had some force to cause so much bruising.'

'Is there respite care available to give them a break away from each other?'

Jo shook her head.

'It's quite expensive and she hates spending money—his money, mind you. That's why she's been bringing him here. She knows we do it on a short-term basis and it costs nothing. The ideal would be for him to sell his cottage and move into an assisted living place called Rosemary House. He'd have his own small studio apartment, all meals provided and his laundry and cleaning done once a week'

'But it's a place you have to buy into?' Charles guessed, and Jo nodded.

'He doesn't want to sell the house, he wants it to go to Barb and her family, but while he's still alive, he insists it's his house, not hers.'

'So Jo to the rescue!' Charles teased.

'Not really,' she said. 'I just happen to know someone who could do with the work and wouldn't mind filling in. It's a small place, Port Anooka.'

Charles was laughing as a white-faced nurse appeared in the doorway,

'It's Schoolies, three of them, drug-affected,

hyperthermic—I've put them in the quiet room, although they're none too quiet.'

Charles glanced at his watch. Nearly seven, but surely too early for these youngsters to be drug-affected.

'Do we know what drugs are most commonly taken?' he asked Jo as they hurried to the treatment room.

'Ice is in epidemic proportions, but younger ones tend to stick with MDMA. They call it Molly and it makes them feel they can dance for ever—which is where the hyperthermia comes in. They'll have been treated at the first-aid tent with cooling packs, and been washed down. The ambos could have started a cold crystalloid infusion, but they are still likely to be excitable.'

'Which means?' Charles asked.

'Sedation, just until we get their core temperatures down. Ketamine is useful, or benzodiazepines can help.'

The youngsters, all women, had arrived in two ambulances, so the room appeared to be full of ambos.

Jo quickly checked the handover details, all three already having been treated with cold packs and had drips running into them.

'Didn't want to go the sedation route until you'd seen them,' one of the ambos said.

The nurses were exchanging the cooling pads

for fresh ones from the freezer. Two of the patients were pale and quiet while one kicked and struggled against the restraints that still held her secure on the ambulance stretcher.

'I suggest we sedate her before we move her to our bed,' Charles said. 'If she gets her hand on the drip she'll rip it out for sure.'

The young woman was cursing and swearing at them, refusing to admit there was anything wrong with her and wanting to get back to the party.

But all three needed cardiac and blood oximetry monitoring, at least until their temperatures returned to normal.'

'Ketamine?' Charles said to Jo.

'I think so,' she said, looking up from the patient she was tending but leaving it to Charles to work out the dose.

Once sedated they moved the third young woman easily, and within minutes they were all hooked up to monitoring equipment and peace was restored.

But although Jo had left him to it, Charles knew there was a lot more to do. He ordered blood tests for all three. With free bottles of water being readily available, all three of his patients could have been drinking copious amounts to cool down before a seizure in one case and a complete collapse with the other two had meant they'd been taken to the first-aid tent.

So their sodium levels could be well down, and that in itself could cause heart arrhythmias, coagulation factors and multi-organ shutdown.

He waited until the blood-test results came through, gave orders to the nurse he was leaving to watch them, and aware from the increased noise levels that the ED was now very busy he went out to discover where he could be most useful.

'I'm beginning to think there was a bad batch of MDMA out there at Port.' Lauren had caught him before he got as far as the triage desk. 'Are your three calm?'

Charles nodded.

'Good. I'll send someone to shift them to cubicles because there's a very distraught patient on his way in. Seizures, hallucinations, the lot! You'll manage?'

'Of course,' Charles said, although it hadn't really been a question, more of a statement of her confidence in his ability.

CHAPTER TEN

'DO YOU NEED a hand?' Jo asked, when she met him outside the calm room at ten. 'Things have settled down somewhat and I'm no longer needed.'

'I've only my patient in the quiet room, but I'll stick around until someone's available to take him over.'

'Takeaway tonight?'

'Sounds like a great idea, you choose the menu,' he said. 'I should be through here before too long.'

'I got a spare flat key today so we can each have one. I'll go across and open the place up to let some fresh air in, then get us something nice for dinner.'

Discussion of the day and their various patients was the conversational focus during the meal.

Nice, safe conversation, Jo thought. And sitting opposite Charles at the small dining table was distracting, but not as distracting as if they'd been touching.

Since they didn't have a cat, she was reasonably sure it was his foot that rubbed gently up her calf from time to time and sent shivers down her spine.

But Charles had mentioned Dottie earlier, and Jo knew he had questions, so when they took their coffee into the sitting area of the small flat she knew she'd have to answer them.

Still, it was better than the conversations about attraction and lust and love...

'Is she struggling for money?' Charles asked, and Jo knew who he meant.

'She has a pension,' Jo explained, 'but I imagine the rates and land tax eat up most of it. Bertie loved the place, and she's been determined to keep it, although the house is falling to pieces and the roof leaks—as you know.'

'But there must have been money in the first place for them to own the house and all the land around it.'

Jo nodded.

'Then Bertie had the stroke,' she said, 'and Dottie wanted only the best of care and attention for him, and that's expensive.'

'So you stay with her from time to time not because it suits you but to see she's not starving to death! This is ridiculous. I can give her money—only I doubt she'd take it. And if she'd

read the letters she'd know there was money from
my mother for her.'

Charles was so agitated he'd stood up and was
pacing the room, disbelief vying with concern on
his strong face.

Jo stood, and stopped his pacing with a hand
on his shoulder.

'She's a very proud woman.'

'Very stubborn more like!' Charles said, resting his forehead on Jo's as he let out a long sigh.

And although they were still discussing Dottie,
somehow his arms were around her waist and he
was drawing her body close to his.

'You've had more practice with her,' he said
against her cheek. 'How do you get away with
doing things around the house and providing
food?'

Jo eased back a little so she could smile at him.

'I tell her I'm going to buy it—the house—
when she's gone so I need to keep it liveable.'

'And are you?'

His dark eyes, looking into hers, were serious
and she knew there was more going on behind
this conversation than Dottie and the house on
the bluff.

'Never in a million years,' Jo admitted. 'I'd
never be able to afford it, but Dottie doesn't need
to know that.'

'I thought as much,' Charles said, as he drew

her close again. 'You are one very remarkable woman.'

The kiss seemed to emphasise his words, as if a remarkable woman needed a remarkable kiss, but no sooner had his lips touched hers than Jo was lost—abandoned to the delight of his mouth on hers, his body pressed against her, his hands in her hair, fingers trailing down her neck.

It was a kiss that fired up every nerve in her body, so her skin and the flesh beneath it came vibrantly alive. His lips explored her face—temple, eyelids, ear—while hers slid down his neck, tasting the maleness of him, wanting him, although she knew it couldn't be.

But this kiss had altered their relationship because now she wanted only to be near him and as he dragged her down onto the couch and put an arm around her shoulder, snuggling her closer, she knew he'd felt it too.

Just to touch, explore, with fingertips and kisses—to be one, bodies merging.

'I'm here for another five weeks,' he said, when they were both so tired they'd been drifting in and out of sleep right there on the couch.

'And I'll still have baby flab,' Jo told him gently.

'Which will not worry me,' he declared. 'Not one iota!'

'But then you'll be gone,' Jo reminded him.

'You could come,' he said, holding her tightly again. 'I'd show you Europe!'

Jo shook her head.

'I rather doubt it's seemly for a prince to be dragging his mistress around Europe with him.'

'I wouldn't be the first,' Charles told her, but Jo shook her head.

'I don't think it's quite me,' she said, kissing him as she spoke, then easing back to look deep into his eyes. 'I'm not that person, well dressed and worldly, able to find enjoyment in doing nothing more than smiling at photographers. Besides, it just isn't practical. I've got to get Allan Bell sorted out and Dottie's roof fixed, and my locum's due to finish, so, thanks, but I don't think so.'

She kissed him again, stopping the protest she could see on his lips, then stood up.

'I'm off to bed,' she said. 'If you thought today was busy, there's always the knowledge that tomorrow could be worse.'

Tomorrow *was* worse, as were the tomorrows after it. For a start, the woman Jo thought would be happy to spend time at Allan Bell's wasn't well and needed care herself.

She thought of moving in herself—a cowardly thought that would remove her from Charles's presence in the flat and the chaos *that* was causing in her body. But with work, she'd hardly ever be there, and Barb had enough cronies among the neighbours to know.

It was Allan himself who solved the problem, popping in to the ED to talk to her.

'I've been talking to a friend whose son's a builder and he says he can have a bathroom installed at the back of my garage by New Year. Then I buy a fridge and microwave for out there, and tell Barb her family can come, but only one family at a time, and they have to camp in the garage. Mostly they go out for meals but they can eat with me, just not be under my feet all the time.'

'That's brilliant, Allan. That way you get back on good terms with Barb, and her family will all get their holiday. There are four more weeks of summer holidays after Christmas so they can take turns to come.'

'And better still I'll have the builders here until New Year to keep an eye on me, so you needn't be worried. And my friend's wife says I'm to have Christmas dinner with them.'

Jo beamed at him, pleased because he'd sorted this out by himself, which certainly disproved Barb's contention that he was losing it.

'It's a great solution,' she said to Charles that evening as they walked home from the tapas bar that was fast becoming their regular eating place.

'And this friend of Allan's can really get it done in such a short time?'

'Apparently,' Jo said, feeling his hand take hers and hers actually nestle into his palm.

Damn it all! She was trying to stay aloof from Charles's not-so-subtle influence over her body and here was her own hand nestling, of all things.

Not that she removed it…

But was he feeling the strain of this not quite real relationship that he suggested a walk before they turned in?

'Have you followed the path out the back?' he asked, and she smiled in the darkness.

'Not for a very long time,' she said.

'Then let's go.'

He led her around their flat to where the path began and, hand in hand, they wandered down towards the sea, hearing it long before they saw it.

'It's so beautiful,' she murmured as they stood on the clifftop where they could listen to the soft shush of the small waves washing against the cliff and look out across the shining ocean.

'It's a magic place!' Charles replied, then turned her in his arms and looked into her face.

Not kissing her, just looking—sighing—then turning to the ocean once again.

Could it be that his mother had implanted a love of the sea deep within him that he was so drawn to it in all its moods—marvelling at its power and strength and beauty?

But what had drawn him to the woman who watched it with him?

Surely not some part of a romantic hangover from his father's tales of love.

Was he subconsciously trying to replicate those stories?

Not that there was anything subconscious in his attraction to Jo!

He put his arms around her and held her close, aware that what he felt for this woman grew stronger every day, and certain that the feeling wasn't one-sided.

But something held her back!

Oh, she joked about pregnancy flab, and he knew now was the not the time for a physical affair, but her response to his kisses told him one thing, while the distance she could put between them left him puzzled.

And not knowing the answer, he made do with a kiss, just to confirm he was right about her response, which, when they finally broke apart, left him breathless and aching for her.

The walk back to the flat was much slower than the walk out to the ocean, both needing to touch and be touched, both needing—no, both greedy for—the sensations their kisses produced.

'You can use the bathroom first,' Jo whispered

to him as they reached the flats. 'I need to pop over to the hospital to check on something.'

By which she meant, *You cool down first and I'll just stay out of the way so we can go off to our separate bedrooms as if those kisses never happened.*

He smiled at her in the glow from the security light above their flat, and brushed her lips with one last kiss, then headed inside to contemplate celibacy, and wonder how some men managed it.

Christmas was fast approaching and by chance— or perhaps because they weren't regular staff— both she and Charles had three days off for the festivities.

'So back to Dottie's this afternoon,' Jo announced at breakfast. 'Hopefully we'll get off work on time so we're not too late getting out there. I've let her know we'll be back and I could almost hear a little excitement in her voice so maybe she's missed us.'

'Missed you, I'm sure,' Charles said, coming out of a little daydream where he and Jo breakfasted together every day—if possible for ever.

For all she responded to his kisses, and often was the instigator of them, she cut off from him if he talked of the future.

And knowing by now how open and honest Jo was, he knew there was some deep reason for her stepping back—for drawing a line between now and whatever lay ahead.

But he had a little time to think for Christmas was upon them.

'So, Christmas Eve, that's tomorrow, we shop,' Jo said as they drove back to Dottie's place, Charles looking forward to seeing his grand-mother and feeling the warmth of the old house after the sterility of the flat.

'Christmas Day we cook and eat and sleep it all off,' Jo continued, 'then Boxing Day is a day of rest.'

Jo was talking so she didn't have to think about Charles in the seat beside her—too close by half—as whatever it was between them seemed to intensify by the minute, or perhaps by the second...

'Cook?' he said, resting a hand lightly on her knee and sending her heart into palpitations.

'Turkey, ham, crispy potatoes done in duck fat. I have it all ordered, we just have to collect it tomorrow and get the pudding, fruit and veg-etables.'

'You're going to cook a turkey in weather that's just about touching one hundred degrees? In Dot-tie's ancient range?'

'And a ham and vegetables,' Jo corrected him. 'It's tradition.'

'It's tradition in Europe where there's probably

a foot of snow outside the door, but here? Why don't we just have a salad?'

'Because it's Christmas!' Jo told him, pleased he'd moved his hand to wave it around in the air to show his disbelief.

He shook his head then rested his hand on her shoulder—which sent her heart fluttering again.

She did wish they would stop, all these reactions to this man.

Or did she?

Weren't they both enjoying their attraction, and what harm could it do?

Apart from leaving her a mess when he departed…

Charles tried to imagine a traditional Christmas dinner served in the Australian summer, and decided he'd just have to wait and see, and in the meantime he had a little shopping of his own to do.

Like his father with Margaret, he hadn't spent long with Jo, but the more he saw of her, the more convinced he was that she was the woman for him. She was intelligent, outspoken when she needed to be, fiercely loyal and protective of those she cared for, and so beautiful she still took his breath away when he caught sight of her unexpectedly around the house or hospital.

While the attraction between them, which

he spent a lot of time trying *not* to think about, would enrich their union enormously.

So he'd slip away from discussions on the turkey that were sure to take place in the butcher's to see what the shops of Anooka could provide for him.

The day arrived, and although Charles baulked at shelling peas in the stiflingly hot kitchen then peeling mounds of potatoes—'There are only three of us!' he'd protested—he began to enjoy the preparations taking place.

Dottie herself had cooked the morning eggs, telling both her visitors not to eat too much toast as they had to keep room for lunch, but she'd then departed, muttering something about wrapping presents, which he'd already been told would be unwrapped after lunch.

'And after that,' Jo said, 'we lie around in a soporific stupor, due mainly to over-indulgence in sub-tropical temperatures.'

Charles had smiled at the image, although he understood they would probably do just that.

It was two in the afternoon before they sat down, by which time a south-easterly sea breeze was blowing through the windows, bringing much-needed relief from the heat.

The table was set with silver cutlery, and shining silver vegetable dishes overflowing with goodness were placed around a beautiful arrangement of vivid red poinsettia.

'Charles can carve,' Dottie decreed, adding, 'That's always assuming you know how to carve a turkey.'

He winked at her, his years following the housekeeper around coming in handy.

Jo passed him plates, and he placed slices of both turkey and ham on them, Dottie complaining that there was no roast pork.

'For just three of us, Dottie,' Jo said, 'I think I've already over-catered.'

But once they'd laden their plates with vegetables, gravy and cranberry jelly, even Dottie conceded there'd have been no room for the pork as well.

They pulled the white and gold crackers set in front of each place, donned party hats, and read silly jokes, sipping ice-cold French champagne Dottie had unearthed from somewhere.

As they ate the delicious meal, Dottie reminisced about Christmases past, Jo made sure everyone had enough to eat, and Charles felt he'd found a place where he belonged—that this was family.

Had Dottie guessed at his thinking that she said, 'Tell us about Christmas at your place.' He did, starting with the enormous tree the staff erected in the front entrance, the fresh pine smell of it and the branches that decorated the banisters rising on either side of it.

Of the formal red and gold dining room, and the international visitors and relatives from other countries who usually graced the dinner table.

'But we eat as we ate today, although our dessert is the traditional pudding, carried in wreathed in flaming brandy, but I think for here, the ice cream one was fantastic. As full of Christmas flavours as the ones we have at home, but without the heaviness.'

He paused for a minute, then added, heart in mouth, 'But you will see, for you will come next Christmas, no? To see the snow and ice and people skating instead of surfing. Come earlier, in fact, Dottie, to see the magic of our autumn leaves, come sooner even, whenever you are free.'

Had he said the wrong thing?

For long moments he waited, then finally Dottie said, 'And Jo? Is she invited?'

His turn to hesitate. He knew he wanted to say that by that time he hoped Jo would be there, because the thought of being separated from her for a full year was more than he could bear.

But that was between him and Jo, so he settled for, 'Of course!'

And the conversation ceased.

'Why don't you two move to the living room

while I clear the dishes away?' Jo suggested. 'Then it will be present time.'

Charles felt as if a giant fist had grabbed his gut and was squeezing hard.

Had he chosen wrong?

Would she be embarrassed?

He held Dottie's chair for her and carried her champagne into the front room, where he discovered stacks of presents set beneath the crystal baubles on the tree.

Jo returned and began proceedings by handing him an enormous parcel.

He opened it to find a beach towel like an Australian flag, and rubber slip-slops also emblazoned with the flag—underwear, board shorts, a T-shirt and even a hat—all Australian souvenirs.

'That's so when *you* come back, you'll have the right gear,' she teased, although he'd never seen such a blatant display of Australiana at the beach.

He parcelled it up.

'I shall treasure it,' he said, catching her gaze and holding it, so she knew he meant it, because even in fun it came from her.

He was watching the blush creep up her cheeks when Dottie handed Jo a present—a small box, wrapped and tied with ribbon. Jo opened it cautiously, then gasped, and said, 'Oh, no, Dottie, that's far too good for you to be giving to me.'

Her fingers trembled as she drew the object

from the box, revealing a delicate gold necklace, set with sparkling sapphires the exact blue of her eyes.

'Put it on,' Dottie ordered, but Jo shook her head.

'It's far too precious and I'm all hot and sweaty from the kitchen.'

'Fiddle-faddle. Jewellery is made to be worn,' Dottie told her. 'They were my mother's and should have gone to Maggie, but maybe they'll go to Maggie's granddaughter someday!'

'Dottie, I can't—we can't—I won't—'

Her old friend smiled knowingly at her, and as he was closest, Charles took the necklace from Jo's trembling fingers and fastened the clasp at the back of her neck, his fingers trailing on the pale skin beneath her upheld hair.

'My turn,' she said, one hand on the jewels, her voice still shaky from surprise. 'Mine to you pales in comparison, but I couldn't decide between buying you another dozen buckets or getting someone in to do the roof.' She smiled as she spoke. 'A patient of mine owes me a favour, and he's starting on the second of January.'

She handed Dottie a card that probably held the written promise.

'Busybody!' Dottie said, but even Charles could see she was pleased.

'My turn,' he said, and they both turned to him.

'But you're a guest, you don't have to give us presents,' Jo protested, but he'd already passed across his presents.

Dottie opened hers, admired the snow scene and red robin on the card, then opened it.

'It's an open plane ticket so you can come whenever you like,' he said. 'Whenever you like, and as often as you like, and stay for as long as you like.'

'Is yours the same, Jo?' Dottie asked, but Jo's hands were shaking too much to open it.

'Later,' she said, and left the room.

Dottie and Charles watched her go, then Dottie turned to him.

'I have something for you,' she said. 'An apology for one thing, to you and your father and most especially to your mother. But you came here looking for her and this is the best I can do.'

She pulled an old red box out from behind the couch, pushed it across the floor towards him, then stood up.

'There's your mother,' she said, her voice thick with tears as she beat a hasty retreat towards the door.

Jo, the unopened card thrust into her pocket, cleaned up the kitchen then returned to find them gone.

'In here,' Charles called, and she found him in

the dining room, sitting at the table with piles of papers spread out in front of him.

'My mother's letters,' he said, his voice charged with emotion. 'Right from when she went away to boarding school. Dottie kept every one of them. And look, see these, date stamps on them—from when she went away—unopened but still kept.'

He had spread out the envelopes along the table.

'Count them. She must have written every week, although Dottie never replied, and here, that must have been when she died, because that's my father's handwriting.'

Jo looked at the unopened letters sorted by date on the table, and put her hand on Charles's shoulder.

'Can you handle this?' she asked, and he nodded—looked up at her and smiled.

'Don't you see, through this gift my mother will come to life for me.'

It was Jo's turn to nod, although those unopened letters bothered her, seeing them set out like that.

'There has to be a reason,' she muttered. 'It can't only be her running away!'

But Charles didn't hear her, so engrossed was he in the rather untidy letter that had been his mother's first one from her boarding school.

Aware he needed to be alone with these treasures, Jo went up to her room, intending to rest, but those letters had been kept—treasured, even if left unopened. Why?

She slipped downstairs as the faintest glimmer of an idea began to take shape in her head. Dottie was resting, Charles discovering his mother—neither would miss her.

She drove swiftly to the hospital and walked into the administration area, greeting the few people she saw but heading for the archives. She'd been here before, seeking information on the parents and grandparents of one or two of her patients, working out whether their problems could be genetic.

Bertie had had a stroke—he would have been admitted here before being transferred to Sydney, so somewhere here she'd find a date.

Supper was a casual meal, out on the bluff beneath the shady tree—leftovers and salad spread on the table for the three of them to pick at.

'And where did you scoot off to in your little car?' Dottie asked as Jo threw a cover over the remaining food and they all lay back in their chairs to enjoy the colours of the sunset reflected on the ocean and watch the first stars show their gleams.

'I went to the hospital, Dottie, and confirmed something I'd been thinking.'

She reached out and took Dottie's small hand in

hers. 'Since Charles arrived, the puzzle of Maggie's disappearance from your life began to drive me mad. I knew it wasn't in your nature to turn your back on anyone, let alone a beloved daughter, and, no, don't shush me, because I think it has to be said.'

'Not if Dottie doesn't want to talk about it,' Charles said, firing up in defence of the grandmother he was still coming to know.

But Jo ignored him, waiting, watching the older woman, who was looking out to sea.

And caught the faintest of nods!

Jo turned to Charles this time.

'I went back through the hospital records and checked the date of Bertie's admission after his stroke. It was the day after your mother left.'

'And you blamed my mother?' Charles asked, but gently, without any hint of judgement.

Dottie shook her head and Jo squeezed her fingers.

'Knowing Dottie as I do, I believe she was more afraid that your mother would blame herself—that Maggie would think the argument they'd had and her leaving home had caused her father's stroke, and Dottie didn't want her carrying that burden.'

'Of course I didn't!' Even softly spoken, the words were vehement! 'How would she have felt? And how could she carry such a burden into whatever new life she'd found?'

'But she'd have come back—helped you, I'm sure,' Charles said, and Dottie turned to Jo.

'It's your story, you tell it.'

'I think,' Jo began, uncertain now about her theory but determined to get it out, 'that with Bertie close to death and the flight to emergency care in Sydney and the long battle to keep him alive that followed, he *had* to become Dottie's priority. She had to be strong for him and if she started thinking about the loss of Maggie it would undermine that strength. Even reading a letter would open up the wound in her heart that was Maggie, and weaken her resolve. Answering a letter—that would be impossible without telling Maggie about her father's illness and causing Maggie distress.'

Charles nodded slowly, then got out of his chair to kneel by Dottie's side.

'I cannot even imagine the pain you must have felt,' he said, 'but I've read the letters—my mother's letters—and in every one she said she loved you and her father and regretted the pain she'd caused you. But she also said she understood there'd be a reason why you couldn't write, because she could never doubt your love for her.'

Silence stretched between them until Dottie was the first to swipe at the tears on her face.

'Well, I hope you're happy, Jo, making us all cry like this on Christmas Day!'

Charles stood up from where he'd stayed kneeling, his arm around his grandmother's thin shoulders.

'Shall I make you some cocoa before bed?' he asked, helping her as she began to stand up.

She nodded, and allowed him to hold her elbow all the way back to the house.

'You can bring it up,' she said, as she climbed onto her own private rocket.

And, thus dismissed, he went through to the kitchen to fix the nightly drink.

Jo had stayed out on the bluff—deliberately, he thought—and although his heart was filled with love for her and what she'd done, he knew his first duty, right now, was to Dottie.

Upstairs in her bedroom, she was already in bed, the Chinese robe like an empress's gown around her shoulders.

He set the small table over her knees and handed her the cocoa, then hesitated, aware there was more to be said, but also aware that she must be emotionally exhausted.

'Sit a minute,' she said—a plea rather than an order this time.

He sat.

'So?' she asked.

'Do I believe that's what happened?'

She nodded.

'It makes sense to me, Dottie, and nothing else did. I've been around you long enough to know you're kind and caring for all your gruffness, and I know you're loyal to a fault. At the time of my grandfather's stroke, you knew your first duty was to him. And if you'd thought about my mother going off you'd have been torn in two and so not able to give him what he needed from you right then.'

'It broke my heart,' she said, 'but I just didn't have the strength to worry about both of them. I chose Bertie and hurt your mother.'

'But I think Jo was right. Telling her would have hurt her even more—she would have blamed herself.'

Dottie sipped at her coffee, nodding slowly.

'It hurt me more than you can ever know,' she said quietly, then she handed the empty mug to Charles and said goodnight.

CHAPTER ELEVEN

EMOTIONALLY DRAINED, CHARLES walked back onto the bluff. He put out his hands to grasp Jo's and pull her out of her chair.

'You are the kindest, most amazing, perceptive and wonderful person I have ever met. I love you, Jo. It's not just attraction, I know that, and I think you do too.'

And almost without conscious thought, he dropped to his knees, her hands still in his, and said, 'Marry me!'

'Silly!' the woman he'd just proposed to said, tugging at his hands to get him back on his feet. 'That's just silly! You're in an emotional whirl after all that stuff came out and it's gone to your head. I've told you already I'm not who you need. You need a princess at the very least, not a country doctor from a very small village in Australia. There must be dozens of spare princesses roaming Europe—beautiful, sophisticated young women who speak half a dozen languages and will do you proud.'

He was on his feet now, his arms around her, looking down into her lovely face as she spoke this nonsense.

'I don't want them, I want you,' he said, and then he kissed her.

'And I think you want me too,' he murmured, when he'd recovered a little breath after the fervour of her response.

He felt her body tremble and the shake of her head against his.

'No, Charles,' she said, and a cold certainty crept through him.

'You mean it?'

She nodded this time.

'I do, Charles, I really do.'

But there was a deep sadness in her voice, and when he tilted her head he saw the tears glistening in her eyes.

'Tell me you don't love me,' he said, speaking gently because he knew there was something very wrong about all of this.

She shook her head, then gave a little huff of cynical laughter.

'I can't do that either,' she said. 'You are the most remarkable man I've ever met. You can bring my body to life with a touch or even a look.

You have made me happy in a way I've never felt before and, yes, I love you, but I can't marry you.'

She tried to edge away but his arms tightened around her, holding her against his body, not kissing her but wanting her close to him, in his arms, as if through the contact he would work out what was wrong.

Finally, by some unspoken agreement, they both turned and walked in silence along the cliff, then into the scrubland where they'd cut the Christmas tree.

Back at the chairs, as he prepared to fold them and return them to the garage, he had to ask.

'Will you tell me why?'

Jo looked at him for a long moment, then subsided into a chair, pulling his close so she could hold his hand for strength to tell her story, as well as gain comfort from its warmth.

And there in the moonlight, with the sea splashing on the rocks beneath the clifftop, she began. She owed him that.

'I don't know how much you know about surrogacy but here very few IVF programmes will accept a surrogate who hasn't had at least one child.'

'You'd had another child?' he asked, and she could hear the other questions in his voice— where is he or she now, did the child die, did you give him, or her away too...?

That last bit was the clincher. What kind of

woman gave away her own child? But it was also the nub of the story.

'I grew up in a kind of commune. There are still many of them here and probably everywhere, but it was a place where several nuclear families all lived on a particular parcel of land and worked it, farmed it, living as closely as possible to self-sufficiency. It was great—other kids to play with, dozens of aunts and uncles, as well as Mum and Dad.'

She paused, aware Charles must be wondering where all this was leading.

'Mum died when I was fourteen. My father took it badly. He shut himself away in his grief, isolated himself from everyone, including me.'

'The person he should most have cared for,' Charles said quietly, and Jo nodded.

'Except that Mum's death finished him in some way—he died five years later, but as far as I was concerned everyone was kind. The women made sure we had food to eat, but it was Leon, a relative newcomer to the commune, who understood that what I really needed was someone to comfort me; to hold me and let me cry and tell me everything would be all right. He made me happy and—well, you can guess the rest. I thought it right, when he asked, that I should make him happy too. Looking back, it was stupid, of course. I knew all about procreation—we had every variety of animal around to learn from, but never in my wildest dreams did I consider that what was happening would lead to pregnancy.'

Had her voice broken that Charles stood up and lifted her so he could sit down again with her in his arms, holding her as she told a story she'd only ever told to Gran.

'I thought I was getting fat because I was eating properly again, then Leon left and I was totally lost. I found Gran's address in an old notebook of Mum's and headed off to Sydney. She was wonderful. She took me in and gave me all the real love that I needed. I was going to be fifteen when the baby was born, a child with a child. We talked about options but it always came back to what I could possibly offer a child. I hadn't finished even high school education, had no job prospects and could hardly depend on Gran to support me and a baby.'

She paused, needing to get it said.

'But the worst thing was, Charles, that I really, really, didn't want that baby. I felt it had been foisted on me, and I hated Leon with all the passion an immature teenager can muster. So I gave the baby away. I hope and pray she has a happy life—I have to believe she does. There, it's out!'

Charles held her close, rocking her slightly on his knee, pressing kisses in the little hollow behind her ear, silently telling her of his under-standing.

'But,' he finally said, 'I know you felt you had to tell me, and apart from wanting to find and kill some bastard called Leon who took advantage of you when you were at your most vulnerable, I cannot see what it has to do with marrying me.'

'Oh, Charles,' Jo whispered, sinking deeper into his warmth and comfort, 'of course I can't. You have to marry and have children, it's your duty to do that to protect the family line, and I've known for quite a while that I don't want children of my own. How fair would it be to that child I gave away for me to have more children—half-siblings she would never know? How would she feel about it if she found out?'

'Can't we ask her?' Charles said gently. 'I know most countries have agencies that help birth mothers find their children, and adopted children find their birth parents.'

She looked at him, hoping the despair she felt wasn't clear to read in her eyes.

'I've tried, Charles, registered with all of them, because I've felt so bad—so guilty—about my feelings at the time. It wasn't her fault she was born.'

'And you've never heard from her or her par-ents? Never discovered if she's looking for you?'

Jo shook her head.

'I've read a lot about it and most adopted children don't look until they're older, and usually independent of their parents. But I wrote to her on her sixteenth birthday two months ago. I tried to explain, and sent the letter through the government agency, who would have sent it on to her parents and left it for them to decide whether or not to give it to her.'

'Oh, Jo,' he said, and wrapped his arms around her, feeling the pain she held in every cell of her body. 'I just don't know what to say—how to help—what I can do.'

'Just love me for a little longer,' Jo whispered to him, snuggling into his arms.

They were sitting under the poinciana tree the following day when Jo's phone rang. She glanced at the number, hoping it might be something she needn't answer, because the previous evening's conversation, though cathartic, had left her exhausted.

'My locum,' she said. 'I do hope there's not a problem.'

'Hi Jo,' her cheerful stand-in said, 'there are some people who've just called at the house, looking for you. Should I send them up to Dottie's?'

'Did they say who they are?' Jo asked, totally mystified, and hoping they weren't reinforcements from Barb ready to storm Allan's house.

'A Mr and Mrs Grey, and their daughter Caitlin. They say they'd don't know you but you sent them a letter.'

Jo shook her head.

'I haven't written to anyone,' she said, 'but best you send them up.'

She closed the phone, and stood up.

'Some people coming to see me,' she explained to Dottie and Charles. I'll go down to the house and find out what they want—I shouldn't be long.'

Charles watched her walk away, his heart aching for this stubborn woman he loved so much.

Then something in Jo's side of the phone conversation—'I haven't written to anyone'—struck him like a bolt of lightning, and he was out of his chair and striding across the lawn to catch up with her as a vehicle pulled up outside Dottie's front door.

Three visitors tumbled out, an older couple and a teenager with vivid red hair.

He saw Jo's face lose all its colour and was close enough to hook his hand around her waist to steady her.

The couple introduced themselves, and then the redhead—Caitlin—the mother crying now as she thanked Jo for the gift she had given them sixteen years ago.

Then Jo was crying and the girl was in her

arms, Jo muttering, 'Please don't hate me,' through her sobs.

The girl stepped back so she could look up into Jo's face.

'How could I hate you when you've given me such wonderful parents?'

Then she grinned and added, 'The red hair I could have done without!'

Then Dottie appeared and took in the situation at a glance, obviously having known the back-story of the adoption. She took over what was usually Jo's role in the house and ushered everyone inside, settling them in the living room where the crystals on the tree threw rainbows around the room.

'You all talk,' she said. 'Charles and I will forage for food.'

And with a look that told Charles he had to follow, she left the room.

The Greys had departed, and Dottie was tucked up in bed before Jo and Charles finally had some time alone.

'Well?' he said, and watched her shake her head.

'I can't think straight,' she said, and seeing the pallor of her skin and the exhaustion in her eyes, he knew this wasn't the time to be demanding an answer to his proposal.

'Go to bed,' he said, taking her gently in his arms and dropping soft kisses on her hair. 'Would you like some cocoa to help you sleep?'

She shook her head and smiled at him.

'There's just so much to take in that I might never sleep again, but I'm so tired, Charles, I'm sorry.'

'Don't be silly,' he said gruffly. 'We've plenty of time to talk.'

And he walked her to her bedroom door, opened it, kissed her goodnight and closed the door.

But for all that nothing had been said, his heart beat with a new happiness. Meeting Caitlin would surely put Jo's mind at rest over having children in the future, and he took himself to bed, to dream of little redheaded children cavorting around the palace.

The ringing phone woke the household at three in the morning, and Jo, used to emergency calls at odd hours of the night, was the first out of bed to answer it. She'd barely worked out what the accented voice was asking when Charles appeared beside her.

'I think it has to be for you,' she said, and passed him the receiver, although she stayed close beside him, holding his free hand, as he answered.

She recognised the words he spoke as French,

but it was his voice that told her the matter was urgent.

'What is it?' Dottie called from the top of the stairs, as Charles replaced the receiver.

'My father,' he said. 'He has had a heart attack. They have done a triple bypass, using stents to open up his blood vessels, but although he is recovering well, I must go home.'

A faint sigh came from the top of the stairs, then a bump as Dottie slid to the floor.

Jo raced towards her, beating Charles by inches, but Dottie was sitting by the time they reached her, shaking her head.

'So silly,' she muttered. 'I never faint.'

There was a pause before she added, 'But it was like history repeating itself. You must go home, Charles, of course you must. Go with Jo and make the arrangements.'

'Not until you're safely in bed,' Jo told her, as Charles lifted Dottie to her feet, then swept her up to carry her to her bedroom.

'And the arrangements are already made,' he said. 'The consul here will organise a plane to fly me back to Sydney first thing in the morning, and they have booked flights home for me from there.'

Jo was checking Dottie's pulse, satisfying herself that her old friend was all right.

'I'll sit with her a while. You go and do whatever you have to do. If that was someone official calling, you might get more information from someone closer to your family.'

'I might have heard it from them if I'd actually charged my phone. I spoke to my father only twenty-four hours ago, phoning him to wish him a merry Christmas, then left my phone by the bed and didn't charge it.'

'Well, do it now,' Jo said. 'Presumably someone local will ring you to let you know when the plane will be here.'

Charles nodded, bent to kiss Dottie's cheek and left the room.

'You could go with him,' Dottie said to her. 'Your locum's booked for another two weeks.'

Jo shook her head, although her whole being longed to be with him on that journey, offering whatever comfort he would accept.

'It's not my place, Dottie,' she said. 'And if his father's had a bypass there should be no risk of another problem at the moment.'

Then Jo bent and kissed her old friend's cheek.

'Try to sleep,' she said, 'and keep in mind that now Charles has found you, you'll be seeing him again. You have the ticket—you could be off to Livaroche next week!'

'You have a ticket too,' Dottie said sleepily, as Jo went quietly out the door.

Charles was waiting for her at the bottom of the stairs.

'This is not how it should be,' he said quietly. 'There is so much we need to talk about, I hate to leave like this.'

Jo put her arms around him.

'But you have to go. Your father needs to know you're there, ready to take care of things until he is well again, and you need to reassure yourself he is recovering, so there's no more to be said.'

'There is much to be said—*so* much—but surely now there is no reason we can't marry.'

'Maybe,' Jo conceded, giving him the lightest of kisses on the thinned line of his lips. 'Let me know when you hear about the plane. I'll take you to the airport.'

His lips had softened so she dropped another kiss on them.

'And say goodbye?' he asked.

But she couldn't answer. Too many things were happening too quickly.

'We'll see,' she managed as he wrapped his arms around her body so they were melded into one.

In the end, Jo broke away, easing herself out of the arms she could have stayed in for ever.

'Go and pack, contact whoever you need to contact, then get some sleep if you can.'

He stood stock still in front of her, his head

bowed, until she put her arms around him in a fierce hug.

One last kiss and she walked away, feeling so bereft she wondered if they did marry, would she feel like this whenever he was called away?

If she *did* marry?

She hadn't allowed herself to think of this for a single instant, but since Caitlin's arrival in her life she knew Charles would see it as the end to any impediment.

But how could she be a princess in a foreign land—learn about protocol and how to speak the languages they spoke and…?

The list grew and grew until finally she fell asleep, totally wiped out by the revelations of the day.

Jo had been back at work four weeks, long enough for the Christmas idyll to be little more than a dream.

Well, a dream and an ache in her heart, made worse every time she spoke to Charles, heard his voice from so far away, and worried for him as he took on his father's duties—for all he assured her it was what he'd been brought up to do!

But he sounded tired and downhearted, and though he spoke of love and missing her, there'd been no talk of marriage.

Dottie had given her a going-away present

when she'd left the big house—two language CDs—one French and one Spanish.

'Just in case he does come back sometime,' she'd said to Jo, 'you'll be able to surprise him. Besides which, I can hardly travel all that way on my own, so you can use that plane ticket and come with me when I go at Christmas to see the snow.'

As if! Jo thought, but didn't say.

Let Dottie have her dream—and Molly could have Jo's plane ticket!

The summer heat departed and on the balmy autumn evenings Jo walked the beach and headlands, reciting the foreign words she'd learned.

Not for Charles, of course, or because she ever intended to visit Livaroche, but it had become a challenge to the extent that once a week she went to the tapas bar in Anooka to practise with real people.

It occupied her mind and gave her little time to brood, so even in the dark of the night when sleep couldn't come, she could run through French verbs or talk to herself in halting Spanish.

She was nearing the end of her afternoon appointments when her receptionist came in.

'Gary Cavill has cancelled but that gorgeous man is here,' the woman whispered.

'What gorgeous man?' Jo asked crossly, pleased she didn't need to have her weekly argument with Gary about wanting heavier opioid painkillers, which she knew he sold for cash in the local pub, but not wanting a new patient.

'The gorgeous man from Dottie's house at Christmas! The one everyone says is her grandson.'

Jo's heart gave an excited little flip, then plummeted to her boots. Did he *have* to come back at the end of a very long day, when she was feeling grubby and tired and probably looked a right mess?

'Send him away,' Jo told her. 'He'll be staying at Dottie's. I can go up and see him later.'

But as the door closed on her receptionist, she wondered if she would.

Her heart still ached but surely the ache had grown less painful? Did she really want to open up that wound?

The door opened to let her flustered receptionist back in.

'He won't go!' she whispered, and Jo shook her head.

'You go,' Jo told her. 'I'll see him in a minute.'

She propped her elbows on the desk and held her head in her hands, aware that hair was escaping from the once neat roll with which she'd started the day, and she must look totally wrecked.

Not that it mattered, the sensible part of her said, but…

She stood up, washed her face and hands, tidied the wildest bits of hair with a splash of water, and marched out into the waiting room.

She was angry now!

What right had he to just walk back into her life like this?

And how pathetic was it that she was practically paralysed with excitement to be seeing him again.

He stood up as she entered, and somehow she ended up in his arms, tears streaming down her face as he patted her back and made soothing noises.

He eased her back a little, produced a spotless handkerchief—probably monogrammed and with a crown over the initials—and mopped her face then smiled at her, and she felt her heart breaking.

'You see,' he said, so gently she wanted to cry again, 'I didn't want to do it over the phone. I wanted to be there, with you, to see your face, touch your hair.'

She frowned at him.

He was definitely speaking English but she didn't seem to understand the words.

'To propose to you!' he added.

Jo felt her legs give way and prayed there was

a chair behind her because she couldn't stand up any longer.

Subsiding none too gracefully, she closed her eyes and tried to think—to sort out what Charles had been telling her. Her eyes were closed because thinking was impossible if she could see him.

Then he was beside her, holding her hand, and it didn't seem to matter what he said because he was here, he'd come back, and somehow everything would be all right.

It was an hour before they got to Dottie's, to meet the housekeeper Charles had brought from his home—the one who'd been his surrogate mother.

And somehow it all got sorted.

Jo would find someone to take over her practice and go back to Livaroche with Charles. And then, come Christmas, when Caitlin had long summer holidays, she and her parents would fly over with Dottie, who had insisted that, first, she would be the one to give Jo away and, second, the wedding could only be held at Christmas because she wanted snow and Christmas lights and—'Would you have a sleigh we could ride in, Charles?'

But Dottie wasn't done with organising.

'You go home with Jo, Charles,' she said, as

the evening finally wound down. 'There's really not enough room here for you.'

'That was telling us,' Charles said as Jo drove him back to her place.

'In no uncertain manner,' Jo said, and knew her voice was shaking. Why wouldn't it? Every bit of her was shaking, and in some distant part of her brain she was glad she'd done so much walking in an effort to forget this man, because at least it had trimmed her body right down.

But as they kissed and held each other, talked and went to bed, it was as if there'd never been any other ending possible for the two of them, as if love always found a way…

EPILOGUE

Jo MET THE Australian contingent of wedding guests at the airport, and drove them—no sleigh today—to the palace, where Charles and his father waited.

If the oohs and aahs had been significant as they drove through the snowy landscape with the streets garlanded with Christmas decorations, it was nothing to the delight with which the enormous Christmas tree in the front hall of the palace was greeted.

But up in the apartment that had been set aside for Dottie—hers for whenever she visited, Charles had promised—there was a small, unadorned Christmas tree.

'Did you bring them?' Charles asked, and Dottie dug into her enormous handbag, producing a carefully wrapped parcel.

'I'll just get my father,' Charles said, and when he came they knelt, just the four of them, and hung the crystal ornaments on the little tree.

For Jo it was the perfect prelude to her wedding—a private time before the very public day that would follow the Christmas festivities. They'd chosen New Year's Eve so the bells that would ring out at midnight would ring in their married life as well as the new year.

The day dawned bright, the sun reflecting off the snow so the whole world seemed to sparkle.

In Jo's bedroom, the clamour of female voices outdid the cooing of the white doves that had magically appeared around the castle, fluttering past doorways and pecking at the windows.

Caitlin and her mother had joined Dottie in helping Jo get dressed—Caitlin already in her bridesmaid's dress of rich blue velvet, a soft white muff dangling from one hand, while Dottie was keeping to the colour scheme in a soft blue-grey dress with a sweeping train.

But it was Jo they were all focused on as she slipped into the simple white velvet gown she'd chosen for the occasion—Jo with her hair swept up in a tangle of bright curls on the top of her head and Dottie's sapphires sparkling around her neck.

'Stand still,' Caitlin's mother ordered, as she climbed on a chair, the better to set a pearl and sapphire comb in the curls, so Jo stood, surrounded by what she considered her family, and fingered the sapphire ring the man she loved had given her. Soon she'd take it off so he could put another ring on her finger, a ring that would bind them together—for ever!

'Sleighs are here!' Caitlin called from the window, where she'd been watching the excitement in the courtyard below.

'Real sleighs?' Dottie asked, and Jo laughed.

'I do hope they're what you wanted, Dottie,' she said, 'because Charles had them especially made.'

She slipped the earrings Charles had given her into her ears and led the troupe out the door, along the portrait-hung corridor and down the winding staircase to where the palace staff had gathered in the entrance hall to wish her well.

Then, holding tightly to Dottie's hand, she walked out to the sleigh, Caitlin and her mother climbing in behind them, while up in front a red-coated driver flicked his whip and six white horses with red plumes on their heads stepped out, drawing the sleigh smoothly over the icy road—especially iced by Charles's decree so Dottie could have her sleigh ride.

They drew up outside the cathedral, and Dottie, as regal as a queen, alighted, then reached out to take Jo's hand. And together they went through the great arched doors, and with the rich, flaring music of 'The Prince of Denmark's March' rising all around them they walked towards the altar, where Charles was waiting, turned towards them, smiling at the pair of them, his grandmother and his bride.

He greeted Dottie first, bending to kiss her cheek before leading her to her seat beside his father, then he turned and took Jo's hand in his, clasping it so tightly she realised he was as nervous as she was.

Until she looked at him and smiled, and saw his eyes light up with love—nerves forgotten in the certainty of the love they had for each other, the love they were about to pledge that would unite them for ever…

* * * * *